Frank Ronan

Frank Ronan was born in 1963 in Ireland. His first novel, THE MEN WHO LOVED EVELYN COTTON, won the 1989 Irish Times/Aer Lingus Literature Prize and was followed by A PICNIC IN EDEN and THE BETTER ANGEL. He has had short stories published in a variety of magazines and in the collection TELLING STORIES 2, and broadcast on BBC Radio 4.

SCEPTRE

Dixie Chicken

FRANK RONAN

SCEPTRE

Copyright © 1994 Frank Ronan

First published as a trade paperback in 1994 by Hodder and Stoughton
First published in paperback in 1995 by Hodder and Stoughton
A Division of Hodder Headline PLC
A Sceptre Paperback

10 9 8 7 6 5 4 3 2

British Library CIP
Ronan, Frank
Dixie Chicken
I Title
823.914 [4]
ISBN 0 340 63244 5

Printed and bound in Great Britain by
Cox and Wyman Ltd, Reading, Berkshire

Hodder and Stoughton
A Division of Hodder Headline PLC
338 Euston Road
London NW1 3BH

DIXIE CHICKEN

A Hero's Death

This is the word of my mouth, the work of my eye, set down so that you may know all that has happened. It is the story of a man who was capable of falling in love. Don't laugh. It is the story of his death, and of those who would have wished to know how he was killed, and of those who were interested in keeping his death a mystery. When Rory Dixon died on me, there was only one person who saw it happen, and that was a furtive, sad individual. No witness came forward when a witness was wanted. It was out on the cliffs above the Black Rock, where the road comes down a steep headland and turns sharply before the land plunges a hundred feet into the sea. Rory Dixon's car came down the hill like a blue streak and sailed out over the cliffs in an arc of music. His stereo was playing that song by Little Feat, full blast. The song about Dixie Chickens and Tennessee Lambs. The black rocks at the foot of the cliff were pointed like church spires, slimy like plastic with the washing of the sea, and one of them skewered the car and held it aloft above the beating water. Rory hung from the car, half within and half without, his hands swinging over the yellow foam. He was unconscious but not yet dead, and there was nothing I could do about it. The wind made him stir a little and the stereo vibrated and the spray washed away what blood had been on him, diluting it pink and

1

running with it from the roots of his hair down to the sea. The rising tide crept higher, swallowing his hands and then his head until, unconscious of what he was doing, Rory Dixon breathed in the water and died of drowning. Under the circumstances there was nothing I could do, neither stop the tide nor raise the car. There are rules for these things and I didn't make them, limitations that even I must acknowledge.

The one person who had seen it all was white with self-containment, knowing that once the weeping started it might be a long time stopping, and he turned for home to await the news of Rory's death.

Early Life

I watched Rory Dixon from the beginning until he was killed. The time I have devoted to him might perhaps have been better used elsewhere, but in recent times I have been observing events rather than interfering in them. And as for time, when I made that, I made plenty of it. Perhaps I should introduce myself. It is a sad reflection of the times we live in that I should need to do so. Most of you will know of me as God, and that identification will have to do for the moment. There are a couple of rumours concerning my person which I should contradict at once. I am not dead and I am not Eric Clapton. I have been silent for a long time. Perhaps I have been sulking, because whenever I have tried to get anything across to you in the past my words have been so badly misinterpreted. In retrospect, those prophets were a lot of airheads, more concerned with the flaming chariot than the job of work I gave them, and I got so disillusioned with the lot of you that I thought I might never speak again. Only the death of Rory Dixon could have brought me out of retirement.

It was the fact that he was born in a cowshed which first drew my attention. There was an echo from the birth of another great charmer in whom I was an interested party. I can sometimes be a little superstitious about these coincidences, so I settled down to watch, appointing myself to be his one-eyed angel. The

3

parents, Brendan and Sheila Dixon, were pre-beatnik beatniks of a sort: hippies a generation before that term had been invented. Sheila was a potter and Brendan a philosopher. They had been living in Dublin, dreaming of a better life, away from materialism and Catholicism and meat-eating and the hollow, inebriated pessimism which passed for intellectual life in that city, until Sheila became pregnant, when they decided that their child should be born in a better place. They bought a cowshed halfway up a mountain on a rough acre and began their wholesome existence, with their kiln and their spinning wheel, and their ideals intact. The cowshed was to be converted, painstakingly, into something they could call home, although by the time of Rory's birth it was still fairly recognisable as a cowshed, if you discounted the piled-up works of untranslated existentialists in the hayrack and the spindly cannabis plants which struggled outside the half-door in the mountain gales. Following their back-to-nature principles to the letter, there was no midwife present at the birth, and Sheila ate the placenta afterwards, and breastfed Rory for the first three years of his life.

He grew precocious on the mountain, falling in ditches and eating cowslips and being woken in the morning by drips of rain that fell through holes in the corrugated roof and onto his sleeping face. It seemed as though he had been given a charmed life and that nothing could harm him. There was the time when he was attacked by a mad dog in Donny Casey's meadow, and the slavering animal had him pinned to the ground, its jaws about to close over his tiny dimpled face. By some miracle, at that moment the dog suffered a brainstorm and died before any real damage was done. Rory pushed it aside, stood up and collected his fallen jamjar, and continued on his way to the pond where there were tadpoles to be captured and where he enjoyed himself with a dedicated thoroughness for several hours. He forgot about the dog until he saw its corpse again on his way home, when he poked at it with an ashplant to see if it was really dead or whether it could be revived. Left to his own devices and with half a mountain to roam over there tended to be incidents of this kind, though not necessarily of this magnitude, most days of the week. He soon learned that the limits of possibility were far beyond the borders of the human imagination, and there was no one to contradict his natural, childish assumption that the only morality was pleasure.

Love was never a problem for him. Sheila and Brendan loved him, if a little absent-mindedly, from the moment of his birth. He was their experiment for a new world order. They set out to prove that a childhood without prejudice or violence or hate would produce a well-balanced, fulfilled adult. He grew to be good-looking and strong, so he was popular with the world outside the cowshed: spoiled by the sugar-beet thinners as they stood about in Dinny Gaskell's field on their tea break with muddy sacking tied to their knees, cosseted by old women in the post office in the village as they bought their weekly quarter pound of coconut creams and lionized by the neighbouring children, who spent their days in the classroom fantasising about his life of freedom in the bracken – all of which is a form of being loved, I suppose. And after puberty he came to be sexually insatiable. So, sex being a priority and having the charm and looks to get it, he had no problem with gratification. And in marrying Helen, he attached himself to a woman who loved him to destruction. So, you see, he was more or less covered as far as love was concerned, in human terms.

But we are getting ahead of ourselves. When he was nine years old he informed his parents that he would like to attend the local national school. His motives were no more than a wish for companionship. He had

5

spent the summer hanging around with the children on Davy Morris's farm, making hay and following the cows home, and the thought of a winter of solitude while his comrades were in school was more than he could bear. The Morris children thought he was mad and described school to him as a hell on earth, but Rory had nothing in his experience which could encompass the idea of hell and their warning made no impression on him. Sheila and Brendan discussed it, and the only great drawback that they could come up with was the danger to him from religious indoctrination. That was over-come by informing the school authorities that they belonged to an obscure Protestant sect and that the boy must be exempted from religious instruction. Any mention of their atheism would have been a disaster, since it would have been an open invitation to the nuns to save the boy's soul from a fate worse than the hell that was reserved for Protestants.

There was also the small matter of the Irish language, which his contemporaries would have been learning for five years and without a knowledge of which Rory would have to be consigned to the Infants' Class until he caught up. Sheila bought the necessary books and, in the last three weeks of August, managed to teach him as much as he would need to know. That was not the extraordinary feat it might seem, since she had already taught him French and German, and languages come easier the more of them that you learn, and since the fluency of nine-year-old farmers' children who have been taught by permanently menopausal half-educated nuns is not of a standard that is difficult to obtain.

There are many children who would suffer if they were sent to school for the first time at the age of nine, but Rory loved it. He was irredeemably gregarious and it excited him to spend the day in a room that was full of people. Because of Sheila's teaching he knew more of maths and geography and literature than the nun herself, so the work was no trouble to him, leaving him plenty of time to observe his fellow inmates. Fortunately a natural tactfulness prevented him from showing off his superior knowledge and his popularity didn't suffer from it. Indeed, he succeeded in charming the withered scrag of a nun so much that by the end of the year he was the only pupil in the school who had escaped a beating, and rather than causing resentment among the other students, with their wealed palms and stinging ears, it made him something of a hero, aided by the fact that his homework was available to anyone who wished to copy it. On paper, this sounds like sickening perfection, but had you met the child you would have forgiven him. Everyone else did.

It was a time of change in the cowshed. From the depths of extreme vegetarianism, Brendan had developed a new theory about the sanctity of eating meat. He had been watching cats eating voles and thrushes eating worms and frogs gorging themselves on dragonflies and finally came to the conclusion that it was the duty of one animal to consume another, and further that it was the sacred birthright of all animals to submit to consumption. Not a man to do things half-heartedly, he refused to eat meat unless he had killed it himself, and he claimed that when you looked into the eyes of an animal at the moment of its death you saw an expression of submissive gratitude, as the beast gave its body to you for your survival. It wasn't long before there were hunks of pig hanging in the cowshed chimney to smoke.

More importantly, he wrote a book about it called *Diet and Karma* which, along with Kerouac, Huxley and Mao, was read with reverence on college campuses around the world, and the cult of the Dixons began. Civilisation began to catch up with the household in the cowshed and, although they were still without running water or electricity, Sheila had an agent in New York who sold her hand-painted-age-of-Aquarius platters for a hundred and fifty dollars a throw. Acolytes from Pittsburgh and the Sorbonne began to turn up at the cowshed looking for enlightenment, and often Rory would come home from school to find earnest hippies sitting at his parents' feet, silent with awe and their own stupidity.

By this time Rory was a well-fleshed meat-fed teen-ager, obsessed by sex, who crossed the mountain every day to the town to attend the secondary school. Most of his contemporaries had begun their working lives, except those who had declared a religious vocation. The lives of those ones were finished. I find it a bit hard that they claimed to have been called by God when I did no such thing, nor would I call such miserable specimens as those. They were called by their own fear. Some were afraid of earning a living and some were afraid of their sexuality and some were afraid of eternal damnation, but not one of them heard the voice of God. I should know. Rory, the only one I had any interest in, was afraid of nothing.

He was an extraordinary thing to look at, and it wasn't only a question of bone structure or stature. It was because he was full of life, and because he was infectious, so that you felt better just for looking at him. And he had that most beautiful mark of all marks possible on the human body. His eyebrows met in the middle.

The idea of being an architect may have come to him because of the privation of the cowshed, which made any other building seem a magical thing. He would question the acolytes about the cities they had come from, never having been to a city himself, and in his innocence he had an ambition to be the designer of the tallest building in the world. A phallic, puerile ambition admittedly, and fortunately one which he kept to himself.

8

Naturally, Brendan and Sheila would have preferred it if he had chosen to be a poet or a weaver, but they were willing to think that if he was to reject the world, as they had, he would have to gain some experience of it first. When the time came for him to take his university place in Dublin, his father knitted him a sweater and he was sent on his way. Sheila and Brendan had plans of their own.

They had, by their own standards, become embarrassingly wealthy, and the spaniel-eyed seekers who turned up at the cowshed were coming in uncomfortably large numbers. It was Brendan who got the idea of going to India to found an ashram, and they moved to the hills of northern Kerala, followers in tow, to squat in the dust and wait for the world to come to its senses. They kept in touch with Rory over the years by letter and by money order, and he visited them once when he was commissioned to build a hotel in Goa, but they never came back to Ireland until his funeral, and having returned to bury him they never managed to get back to India again. They should have stayed there, in Manantavaddi, where they were known and venerated as gods, where they belonged, and left the dead to bury himself.

Again, we have lost hold of chronology; we are jumping ahead of ourselves. Rory and his libido went to Dublin for the first time when he was eighteen, to begin his studies. He was absorbed into the city like charlie in a nostril. He didn't have to go through the stage of being a gauche culchie in the big smoke; there was no awkwardness, no cultural cringe. He knew everything from the outset and became an electrifying presence, fucking and drinking his way through every party and pub between Ballsbridge and the Park gates. He was possessed of enough curiosity to sleep with almost anyone once, and that he could sleep with so many was a mark of his charm, at a time and in a place where few people ever got their end away without money changing hands, or a child being conceived, or both. I admit he had two physical advantages which are not given to everyone. The first was those eyebrows, which made him seem dangerous, untrustworthy, sinful, and so a magnet for those who were bent on sin. His second advantage was the shape of his organ of generation, which tilted downwards towards the end, like the nose of a Concorde airplane, which is the best possible shape for hitting certain mysterious spots deep within the invaded orifice. Word got round, and before long he had as many requests as refusals. And then he met Helen.

I know what you are thinking. No one can be that perfect or charming. You are conceited enough to think that if you had met him you would have been the exception and disliked him. That might have been a problem for him if he had never met Helen. Every great man has to have his flaw and Helen was his. She did him the great service of earning him the sympathy of everyone who met her for the rest of his life.

It started on a libidinous summer night in the early seventies. Rory had been making a name for himself as the young Turk of architecture, and he was out on the sniff with his friend, Andy McGrath. Out on the sniff was their expression, not mine, and it involved a hedonistic ramble through the pubs and dance halls, hunting down girls like a pair of pack dogs, and sharing the quarry at the end of the evening if it was necessary. Often it was necessary, because Andy McGrath was no oil painting and his chief motive for hovering in Rory's wake was to pick up the discards, usually when the girl was too drunk to notice. It was a harmless bit of fun.

On this night, two English girls in silver platform shoes, Helen and her sister, out of their depth in a crowd of serious drinkers, were picked up by Rory and Andy as they were leaving the International Bar.

10

Between one thing and another and one thing leading to another they all ended up back in the girls' hotel room, where Helen coupled with Andy on one of the single beds, while Rory fucked her sister three feet away on the other. Even then Helen loved him and that was maybe why she opted to sleep with Andy. She was afraid of the strength of his attraction, and her instinct told her that once she was sucked in there would be no escape, which turned out to be true. And although it was never spoken of again, her first memory of him remained the sight and sound and smell of him giving pleasure to her sister, while she endured Andy McGrath's flailing and moaning. The spectacle was to haunt her with jealous nightmares until the day of Rory's death.

If the truth is to be known, in the morning Rory was unsure which girl he had slept with, but the two of them were left alone together while her sister was in the bathroom and Andy was out getting a hair of the dog, and Helen looked at him in a certain way, and he looked at her in a certain way, and they were married within the month. Of course there was a lot of talking and sex and soppy walks through Dublin in between, but the business had its roots in that exchange of glances in the Shelbourne Hotel. Because, whether we realise it or not, we recognise our mates the moment they track us down, and most of us bow to the inevitable after that, and call it love.

The Consequences of Marriage

It might seem that the rest of his life was well-documented elsewhere. He was one of those people who seemed famous to those who knew him since his name was mentioned so often in the papers, but there are strings of names in the papers every day of the week, and there are general readers who attach no importance to architecture and who would not have noticed how he became the nearest thing in that profession to a movie star. And memory is bad, and it is often imagined that the person who stands before you has always been the same. There are only a few of us who can remember the line of discarded personae behind that person, and remember the transformations, and guess at the reasons for them.

And it is rare to fall in love at the moment of someone's birth, for that love to gather strength for the whole of his life, and never to know disappointment. Fond parents will tell you that they have known this, but they are deceiving themselves. I was a parent myself, and I know how rare this thing is, no matter how strongly it is wished for. Disappointment is as natural to love as exhalation is to breathing.

But marriage is a catastrophe I have been spared. Whom, in all honesty, can you marry if you are the supreme being? In mythology there are gods who marry their sisters or their mothers or mortals, but

13

who would choose to be Cronus or Uranus or Epimetheus? Whom could you love enough and at the same time despise enough to burden with the curse of being your consort? These complaints, perhaps, have no place here. I have set out to tell the story of another, one to whom I was of no importance, and so I must stay in the background – if I can. Humility will not be easy for one so accustomed to flattery as I, for one who sees no virtue in humility, or in anything.

This marriage, and the transformation of Rory Dixon. There were those who said that it changed him, and that it was a pity. It is true that outwardly he became more conventional. Before Helen, his idea of entertaining a guest was a bottle of champagne and a fresh pair of sheets. Dinner parties followed hard on the heels of her arrival, mitigated admittedly by Rory's hospitality, which meant that his interpretation of the *trou Normande* was a mirror covered with lines of white powder which passed from guest to guest between courses. And naturally everyone was offered a tab of acid with their coffee.

In those first months Helen was suspended somewhere between happiness and bewilderment. At one instant she believed that she loved him so much that she would do anything for him, and at another instant she would find that an instinct to tame him was gnawing at her love. She had not married him for his wildness but despite it, and she felt that if she could deconstruct, carefully, the armour of his energy, she would find the man she loved somewhere beneath it.

On their honeymoon in the Azores, they were joined at dinner one night by a single woman, a Venetian with the marks and the attraction of the debauched, who amused them with her conversation, and who must have recognised some kind of fellowship in Rory, for it was obvious by the end of the evening that she was propositioning the both of them. Helen gave no indication of acquiescence or disapproval and Rory was tempted, but for the first time in his life he resisted the call of pleasure. Afterwards, they were walking arm in arm from the restaurant to their hotel, with the scent of the Atlantic in their nostrils, and Helen broke the silence by saying, 'I would have done it, you know. If you'd wanted me to I would have done it. Did you want to?'

Then he knew why he had resisted the temptation: not out of love, but because he was being tested, and it was the kind of test which he couldn't have dignified with a response.

'Done what?' he said, as though in innocence.

'That woman. She wanted to go to bed with both of us. You must have noticed. I didn't want to myself, but I would have done it for you.'

'Why?'

'I suppose I don't know you well enough. I don't know if that isn't the sort of thing you like doing. If it is, I'm willing to give it a try.'

And although she believed what she was saying at the moment she said it, he recognised the danger of being honest with her, and out of love for her he lied and said, 'You know it's only you I want.' And once he had said it he could feel the rush of her pleasure and her relief, and that was the first transformation of Rory Dixon.

He learned, from Helen, that however much you could get away with by honesty, you could achieve twice as much by being equivocal. He learned that her love was founded on a misinterpretation of his character, and that if he was to keep her love his character must remain coded. That, perhaps, was not a recipe for a marriage which was to last another twenty years, but he was not thinking of the future. He was thinking only of a present in which his most pressing need was to be constantly in her company, and he would have compromised anything to achieve that state.

They returned to Dublin and bought the house in Mountpleasant Square, gutted the interior, replaced the entire back wall with glass and spread enough polished concrete over the surfaces to make it the first minimalist house in Ireland. Helen discovered that she had talents as a publicist, and it was partly due to her that he passed from well-known to famous.

He was never anything but happy. If he ever thought of death it was with a sort of expectant curiosity, even to the extent of playing Russian roulette once or twice. She was dissatisfied by nature, and never thought of death at all, only of escape from him in her wilder moments of fantasy. She felt that he was defeating her and, because it was difficult to put this fear in rational terms, that he was driving her mad.

No marriage is possible. No two people can sustain themselves equally in a union. The best you can hope for is that each will take it in turn to abase themselves before the need of the other. With Rory Dixon this was not possible. He was relentless in the pursuit of his own life and it was up to Helen to muddle along in his wake.

Soon after Corinna, their only child, was born, they found the house at Innish on the Barrow estuary, and that may have been what saved the marriage. For the six good months of the year Helen would stay down there, having Corinna with her in the school holidays and Rory on the weekends when he could get away from work. The beau monde of Dublin would follow them, their intimates taking houses close by and would-be intimates draping themselves around the Commodore Hotel. Rory had more friends than most people have acquaintances. Good, genuine, intimate friends. He was so alive that no one had ever feared for his death. And then the blue car went over the cliff; but that is another part of the story.

Helen loathed being pregnant. It made her feel ugly and powerless, and it was the beginning of her conviction that Rory was unfaithful to her. As she lay bloated on her sofa she convinced herself that no one could love her, and in her boredom she imagined Rory coupling with other women and in her mind's eye she saw his backside clench and shiver as it had clenched and shivered between the thighs of her sister. She began to check on his movements and keep an eye on his mail, but there was no evidence of infidelity. And her conviction was fuelled by the lack of evidence.

When she first began to scream he forgave her, because he had read somewhere that pregnant women were inclined to behave like that. When Corinna was born and the screaming got worse he put it down to post-natal depression, and by the time there were no excuses left for the screaming he had become used to it, as though there had never been a time without screaming and as though the screaming were an integral part of the woman he was in love with.

When Corinna was born and he saw his child, Helen saw undisguised love in his eyes, and that was intolerable to her. She tried to love her child and made all the conventional outward noises of motherhood, but she could never forgive a creature who had caused her such ugliness and pain, who in her own mind had lost her Rory's love, and who had earned Rory's instant love by nothing more than genetic coincidence. The birth isolated Helen completely, and those of Rory's friends who had tried to like her before now tolerated her only for his sake.

I have never seen quite what was so dislikeable about this woman. Perhaps she measured up badly in comparison to Rory. She had an unfortunate manner which was more than mere tactlessness; she was inclined to sulk, and later to scream, in public; she was wary of

17

everyone, since anyone could love Rory and her self-esteem was low enough for her to consider herself easily dispensable. She could be charming, but she could never maintain her charm for a whole evening and most people's meetings with her had ended on a note of rancour. Perhaps, more than anything, it was these betrayals which made her so disliked. Perhaps if she had had no goodness in her at all she could have been more easily accepted.

They remained married. There were those who said that Rory stayed for the sake of the child, but the fact was that he loved her. Not, perhaps, the same love that he had felt over breakfast in the Shelbourne Hotel, but a love that had something to do with loyalty. He was aware that he was, to some extent, responsible for her state of mind. And more than that: there were good moments, in private, when he could watch her move about a room, and know happiness from the watching, and there were bad moments when he could feel the ferocity of her love in her anger; and there was a life which went from day to day and was more good than bad in its entirety; and Rory Dixon was secure enough in his happiness not to be made miserable by the misery of another.

And she stayed with him because she could think of nothing else. Even if she thought of leaving him, she thought of it only in terms of the effect it might have on him. She never got as far as thinking what she would do with herself.

Stretched end to end it was only a life. I am said to be immortal, and that is meant to be a comfort to me, but, as with you, all that it means is that I have no memory of my birth and no experience of my death. I loved and he loved and she loved, and none of us were loved in the way we wanted to be, nor is such a thing possible. There are some things I can't help, even I, nor should I.

Death Unveiled

Moby Donlan and Alan Kehoe had fished the whole day without a word passing between them. The boy Alan had sworn to himself that morning that if the older man opened his mouth he would get a box in the jaw, and Moby knew it, by instinct, and kept his silence. That morning, as he was leaving the house, Alan's mother had told him that she was pregnant. There had been no need to ask who the father was. Moby Donlan had been paying court to her for the past six months, since Alan had left school and started fishing with him. It was a double betrayal, for Alan had lost his mother and his mentor in the same blow, or that was how it seemed to him, which is an understandable way of seeing things at the age of sixteen rising seventeen.

It had been a good day for fish. There were salmon in boxes on the deck and mounds of net that were relatively undamaged. They were coming back along the coast towards Ballinglass harbour, with Alan at the wheel, when an odd blue shape came into view at the bottom of the Black Rock. They both saw it, and studied it as the boat drew nearer. It took the form of a car, impaled on one of the rocks. A blue Lancia Spider, with the body of a man dangling from the open door. The head of the man was below water in the risen tide. Alan brought the boat as close as he could without danger. Moby stood with his back to him, immobile in the bows. Alan knew that Moby couldn't swim. In Moby's day swimming was considered bad luck for fishermen. If your boat was lost it was better to die of drowning below the water than to die of exposure paddling around on top of it. He wanted to shout at Moby to take the wheel, but still he couldn't bring himself to speak to the man, so he let the boat drift for a moment, and when he saw that the current was taking it away from the rocks he left the wheel.

The first thing that Moby knew of it was when he saw Alan, stripped to his underpants, dive past him into the water. He shouted after him, but that was all he could do. In two minutes the boy had crossed the short distance between the boat and the rock.

Even though there was little chance of him being alive, Alan lifted the man's head out of the water. He felt a compulsion to look at the face. It was a handsome, humorous face, charming even in death and cold water. It was the face of a man he would have chosen for his mother, instead of the slob Moby. Moby with his shaking stomach was a good man for a friend and a boss, but not a good man to imagine coupling with your mother. Alan thought these things as he trod water by the corpse, as he had thought them all day on the deck of the boat.

He looked back. Moby was leaning over the side, his jaws agape. Alan thought that he would prefer to stay where he was rather than return to the boat, but at least if he had to go back he wouldn't go alone. He caught the upper arms of the corpse and braced his feet against the rock and pulled. The sharp ridges of rock scored into the bare soles of his feet, and the corpse lolled against him like a friendly drunk, but something was caught somewhere inside the car and there was no downward movement, so he used the corpse as a ladder and climbed over it, leaving a bloodstain on the man's shirt from his cut foot.

It was the sort of car that adolescents dream of. Open-topped and leather-seated. A small clicking noise drew his attention to the centre of the dashboard. 'Auto-Reverse' was spelled out in blood-red lights on the stereo. There was another click and the music began, drowningly loud. It was a song about Dixie Chickens and Tennessee Lambs. God knew how many times it had played and rewound itself since the crash.

He freed the corpse's legs and let it slide from his hands into the sea, diving after it and, using a half-remembered lifesaving technique, towing the dead man back to the boat. It was a slow swim, the weight of the body rubbing against him with a tempo that was nearly sexual. Between the movement of the swimming and the movement of the water the body seemed almost to come alive against his flesh, and he had to concentrate to keep his mind straight and his own body under control. He was a boy who had prided himself on his normality, and neither homosexuality nor necrophilia were in his previous experience. The shock of them both at once would have made him abandon the body to the fishes, but he heard Moby's voice at the same moment and felt the side of the boat against his shoulder. Moby began to haul the man aboard as he pushed from below, panting in the cold.

And then Moby's hand was reaching down for him, but he would have none of that. He wouldn't be touched by hands that had known his mother, that had done God knew what to her. So, with great difficulty, he pulled himself over the side of the boat and lay breathless, side by side on the deck with the man, while Moby revved the engine and headed for Ballinglass harbour.

While he dried himself and dressed he couldn't keep his eyes from the corpse. It occurred to him that the face should be covered, but it wasn't the sort of face

21

you could cover. Although it wasn't smiling, it had a smiling look about it, as though there were still life somewhere beneath it. Death, after all, is usually a great enhancer of charisma.

He had a feeling that Moby was watching him, and seeing something intrinsically private. He turned. 'What the fuck are you lookin' at?' he said. They were the first words he had spoken since morning.

'You know who yer man is?' Moby said.

Alan didn't answer. He neither wanted to know who it was nor wanted Moby to tell him.

'It's yer man Dixon. The architect fella who stops the summer over at Innish.'

Still Alan said nothing, but stared at the face of his corpse, thinking of what a waste it was of a face, and wishing he could see it move. He would have liked to touch it above the bridge of the nose where the eyebrows met, but couldn't with Moby watching.

Moby said something he shouldn't have, in the awkwardness of Alan's silence. 'I heard the boys had it in for him.'

And then, realising he had been indiscreet, he began to prattle. 'We shouldn't have touched the body, I suppose. We should have just told the cops.'

Then Alan spoke. 'He might have been still alive.' He said it almost without opening his mouth, then looked at Moby with such derision, and with such a potential for violence, that the older man was quiet until they were tied up in Ballinglass.

Catherine Mulcahey, Alan's girlfriend, was waiting for them on the pier. Before they could stop her, she had jumped down into the boat and seen Rory Dixon's body. She had never seen one of the dead before, so instead of reacting with horror she knelt on the nets beside the body and stroked the face as if it were a sleeping child.

'What's wrong with him?' she said.

Alan couldn't bear it. The first irrational thought to cross his mind was that he couldn't stand to see someone else touch his corpse. And then he thought that the whole thing might be a trap, and the corpse would rise and laugh at him and inform on him to Catherine, would tell her what had been felt in the water, would shatter his life. What chance could he have of being morally indignant with his mother and Moby once it was known that he had been made horny by a dead man?

He pulled Catherine away and brought her down to the other end of the boat while Moby went up to the pub to call the police.

'What's wrong?' she said. She was frightened now, by his roughness more than anything.

'He's dead.'

She kept her arms around him while looking back at the body. She kept asking him if he was sure the man was dead. He pulled her close to him so that his erection pressed against her hip, and was reassured that he was not a pervert after all.

At about the same time, Sergeant Foley and a young garda called Aidan Connelly were out at the top of the cliff above the Black Rock. A tourist had reported that there was a car at the bottom and they were trying to get a view of it. The sergeant, being a heavy man, wouldn't go too near the cliff edge but sent Aidan ahead of him. Aidan slithered in the sea pinks and stained his uniform with seagull shit. He had grown up near this place and climbed these rocks in his childhood. It was a long time ago, before his family had moved to Dublin, and he was trying hard to remember. He could recall eating a live limpet for a dare and then being ostracised by the disgust of the others for the rest of the day, because they hadn't expected him to go through with it. He couldn't remember if, climbing the cliffs then, he had been so afraid of falling as he was now.

Foley called to him. 'Can you see who it is?'

Aidan muttered as he leaned forward. 'Probably another bloody tourist thought he was on the autobahn.' He craned his neck. 'Jesus, Mary and Holy Saint Joseph.'

'Well?' the sergeant said, coming a small cautious step closer.

Aidan turned his head to shout, losing his grip on the turf for a moment, almost sliding over the cliff and only just recovering himself.

'It's Dixon. It's the blue Spider.'

He couldn't see the sergeant's face, but he would have expected the information to be a great shock to him. When the sergeant answered, in a flat tone, 'You'd better be coming back so, before you join him,' Aidan was surprised by his lack of astonishment. He had thought that the sergeant and Dixon were close. He clawed his way back up the stiff grass to safety and the two of them went back to the squad car to use the radio, looking like Laurel and Hardy from the rear. It was as they reached the car that the call came through to say that Dixon's body had been recovered and was beyond in Ballinglass harbour.

On the drive down from the cliffs Aidan said, 'You're very calm about it.' He knew he was overstepping some sort of mark by talking to a senior officer in that way, but he wasn't in control of himself.

'Am I?' the sergeant said. 'The man drove like a hoor, except he wasn't paid for it. It was bound to happen one of the days.'

Aidan missed a gear change, and there was a terrible grating sound. He knew he should be taking his cue from the sergeant, be professional about it. But it was the first death he had come across where he knew the victim.

24

'I thought he was a great friend of yours,' he said. He could hear the plaintive, almost accusatory tone in his own voice.

'In this job you don't have friends. You know people. And Dixon knew everyone.' The sergeant's voice was too controlled to be plausible, but Aidan could think of nothing else to say. It was true that Dixon had been a fast driver. The sergeant had fixed three speeding charges for him in the last year alone. Aidan knew he was being naive, but if Dixon and the sergeant had a relationship where speeding charges were fixed as a matter of course, why was the man being so cool about Dixon's death? His head was full of questions, but none of them would make themselves into sentences.

Nothing more was said until they reached the harbour and then they were kept busy, asking questions and writing down answers, deflecting questions that they didn't know the answers to, and sorting out who was important and who merely had a sense of their own importance.

It seemed as if people had come out from under stones, and the small village of Ballinglass was black with the curious. The first task was to get people back from the pier and make a path for the ambulance, when it would arrive. The owner of the boat, Moby Donlan, was incoherent, as if he were frightened by what was happening. He kept saying, 'I knew we should have left him alone. I shouted after the lad to leave him alone. It wasn't me thought of it. It was the lad. He's only a lad, I suppose.'

Their best chance of getting the story was from the boy himself, who stood in the bows of the boat with his arms around a girl. She was a clear-eyed creature with bitten fingernails. The boy had such a strange look to him that he looked like a creature from another planet, but Aidan put that down to the shock.

Sergeant Foley would have asked the girl to leave

25

the boat while he asked Alan a few questions, but the boy was holding onto her as if he was holding on to his sanity (and) so the statement was taken without separating the two of them. Alan told his story lucidly, logically and chronologically.

Then the sergeant said, 'Why didn't you ask Mr Donlan before you jumped in the water?'

Alan glanced at his employer, and the glance would have been eloquent enough, combined with Moby's babbling. But he also said, 'Him?' in a tone of voice that made the answer to the question complete.

Aidan stood by the body, being in charge of crowd control. He was shocked by the remains of Rory Dixon, in the first place because he seemed not to be dead, and in the second because it was proof of his death, a fact that Aidan was finding it increasingly hard to come to terms with the more he thought about it. He knelt over Rory to feel his pulse for the third time, picking up one of his hands and looking at the perfect square fingernails. He could feel no pulse, but he could feel electricity, or charm, or something.

He felt a movement behind him and saw that Alan was watching him, having told all he could to Foley and found the courage to set himself adrift from his girlfriend. Alan said, 'Did you know him?'

Aidan said, 'Everyone knew him. He was a nice man. You would have liked him.'

Before he knew what he was saying, Alan said, 'I liked him anyway.' And then he turned away quickly and climbed onto the pier, ashamed of himself.

When at last Dixon had had his face covered and had been put in the ambulance and taken away, the sergeant called Aidan over to him and said, 'You had better take my car and go and inform Herself. I'll clear up things here and get some of the boys to come out and pick me up.'

That was a task that Aidan hadn't considered. His

face fell and he spoke to the sergeant in a pleading voice, like a child who wants to stay up and watch television. 'You know her better than I do. She'll go mad on me.'

'I have work to do,' the sergeant said. 'And you have orders to follow. Now go on, quick, before she hears it from someone else.'

As he was about to get into the car, Alan's face was before him again. He could see that in normal times it would be a face that was luminous with sunburn, a broad flattish face that was built to have a smile across it. But in the present circumstances the boy looked old with worry, and the sunburn made him look creased and foxed, on the threshold of disintegration.

From this face Alan said, 'Do you have any ideas who did it?'

From the way he said it, Aidan felt that he was trusting him with a confidence, and at the same time expressing something that had been at the back of Aidan's own mind: that this event had not just happened, that somewhere behind it there was a human intention. But he was enough of a policeman to be cautious. Nobody, and by that he meant Sergeant Foley, had suggested yet that it was anything other than an accident.

'How do you know someone did it?' He said it gently, with no scepticism in his voice.

'Nothing,' Alan said. 'Moby said something, is all. Moby's ranting anyway. He's off with the fairies.'

Aidan glanced at the back of the sergeant down on the pier. It was a broad expanse of navy blue cloth moving sluggishly among the people, like an old bull in a crowd of heifers without the energy to mount or the humility to relinquish his seigneurage.

'Do me a favour,' Aidan said, still watching the sergeant to make his meaning clear. 'If you think you know anything, tell me about it first.'

He saw the boy in his rear view mirror as he drove away, standing still in the place where he had left him, but Catherine Mulcahey had rejoined him and he had his arm around her again, in an attitude that seemed more like need than pleasure.

The sergeant had been right about the danger of Herself hearing the news from elsewhere, because when Aidan stopped for petrol at Priesthaggard the place was already awash with it, and some of the drinkers came out of the pub to the pumps, glasses in hand, to get details.

'There's nothing known yet,' Aidan said, 'except that Dixon is dead and the car is wrecked.'

'I suppose you'll be saying it was an accident.' Tom Higgins spoke with his mouth half-inside a pint glass.

'What's that supposed to mean?'

'Oh, nuthin'.' Tom Higgins sniggered and winked at the other drinkers.

Aidan was not at his best in front of these men who had been the drinking companions of his father, who had bought him packets of crisps on Sunday afternoons when he was little. The uniform on his back meant nothing to them. He tried to sound officious. 'If you have any information on the case you'd be better bringing it to the barracks than gossiping about it here.'

That made things worse. He wouldn't look in their direction, but he could sense that they were laughing at him.

'There's a case, so?' Tom Higgins spoke with a gravity that could only be mockery.

Aidan got in the car and started the engine in preference to being tempted to an answer. 'I have to go and inform Herself,' he said.

That was one of the few things he could have said which could have purchased him a sliver of compassion. 'Good luck to you, boy. I wouldn't like to be inside a half-mile of that place when she hears.'

Herself

Helen Dixon was at home, looking through her husband's correspondence with the air of a woman who had become used to filling his absences in that way. Before she moved each piece of paper she memorized its exact position in the drawer, so that it could be replaced without any sign of disturbance. If you had asked her what she was looking for she wouldn't have been able to answer you, but she knew that it had something to do with her own sanity, to do with her having been right all along, about everything. In twenty years of marriage there wasn't anything she hadn't accused Rory of. All she required was one shred of evidence which substantiated one accusation, and then her life might be her own again. Her life, for a long time, had consisted of nothing but loving and hating Rory Dixon, of being suffocated by obsessive thinking of him. There were times when she would easily have killed him out of self-preservation, and had only been stopped by that same sense of self-preservation.

She was a thin woman, not naturally thin for she was big-boned, but thin for the sakè of elegance. She was attractive, in a sexual rather than a photogenic way, and she had a brilliant smile on her good days, which weren't many. She would smile when he was making love to her, with her eyes wide open, because she thought that lent honesty to their love-making. But the effect of it was unnerving to him, and the result was that they only made love when he was drunk or stoned, and too far gone to be haunted by her smiling, staring face, and her anxious clinging to him as she came.

It could, I suppose, be traced back to the night they met, when she had watched him with her sister in the Shelbourne Hotel. It could be that she was an old hippy at heart despite her present brittle appearance; that she believed that copulation was primarily a spiritual act, of which the sweat and gristle were by-products. It could be that she loved him too much, and not well enough. She liked him best when he was asleep and she could keep an eye on him.

There was nothing incriminating in his correspondence; there never was. There were business letters and letters from journalists asking for interviews and letters from students asking for placements, and all the usual social and charity stuff. There was a letter from his mother which she read in a cold fury, because there was no mention of herself in it. She had never met his mother, so there was no reason that she should be mentioned in a private letter, which spoke only of plumbago and the near-suicide of a tribal woman who worked at the ashram. But Helen was sensitive to exclusion, and saved this omission in her memory for the next argument. Methodically, she was moving on to the pockets of the jacket he had left hanging over the back of the chair when the doorbell rang. She took her time answering it, checking first to see who it was from behind a curtain. She saw the back of a man in uniform, and assumed that her daughter Corinna was in some sort of trouble again. It was in resignation rather than alarm that she made her way into the hall.

Aidan Connelly waited outside in unprofessional embarrassment. He picked invisible dirt from his uniform with his left hand, while his right hand seemed uncertain whether to remain on the inside or the out-side of his trouser pocket. It wasn't that Innish was what you might call a big house, but it was an imposing one, with a front door designed to send the lower orders scuttling around to the tradesman's entrance at the back. The air was thick with the scent of philadelphus, making him feel queasy. He was beginning to hope that Helen wasn't at home when she opened the door to him.

She greeted him with a hint of affection. She too had known him in his childhood. 'I can never get used', she said, 'to seeing you in uniform.'

Beneath the crisp Englishness of her voice, his own dissolved to a stutter. 'Mrs Dixon, Mr Dixon is dead. The blue car was found this evening at the bottom of the Black Rock. There was an accident, it seems.'

He watched her face, waiting for the scream or the dissolution, but neither happened. Her face was fixed into the smile she had borne for him at her greeting and, instead of going mad, she asked a mad question.

'Do they know who killed him?'

Aidan had the sort of face that lent itself to dumb-foundedness at the best of times. 'Ah, Mrs Dixon,' he said.

When Alan had asked him more or less the same question his response had been sympathetic, but now that it came from the mouth of a known madwoman in shock he was alarmed by it. He didn't feel that he could give any answer which allied himself to her, and he couldn't, for the moment, see any way out of it.

She turned away from him back into the house, and his first thought was that he had fulfilled his brief with relative ease and would have gone away, but he hesi-tated. She had left the door open. She had a remarkable way of walking. He followed her white shirt and her long velvet leggings through a hall like the hall of a gentleman, full of walking sticks and shooting sticks

31

and the mounted masks of foxes that had been hunted by another family and bought in a country house sale, and into a drawing room like the set of an advertisement with chrome and glass furniture and curtains that trailed across the floor. She stood in a window with her back to him. He had never noticed before how long her legs were, and was ashamed of himself for noticing it now.

'Your curtains are very long,' he said, thinking that maybe she had got them second-hand and not had time to take them up yet.

'Fortuny,' she said.

'Better that than the other, I suppose,' he said, thinking that she must have said *fortunately*. He was relieved that her voice sounded as though it were under control, but was apprehensive about seeing her face.

'Can I offer you a drink?' she said.

'I'm on duty.' He said it uncertainly and then looked at his watch. 'Well, I am and I amn't. All right so, I'll have a small one.'

She turned, her face expressionless, and he wondered if the screaming was next. He had only witnessed this screaming once himself, but he had heard of it often. She was said to have performed it in every restaurant in the county, until people wondered how Rory Dixon had the courage to be out in public with his wife at all. The time he had seen her do it was in the pub in Arthurstown. She and Rory were having a quiet drink one minute, and the next minute the place was full of her shrieking voice. It was something like, 'SO WHAT DID YOU DO THEN? I SUPPOSE YOU ROGERED HER. JUST HAD HER OVER THE TABLE, DID YOU?' and so on. You wouldn't say that Rory was embarrassed by it, but he was cowed. His posture fell forward so that he looked like a smaller man, and he drained the drink from his glass and stood up and walked out, nodding sheepishly to the other customers, with the apologetic smile on his lips that people have when their blood has gone cold where it should have heated. She followed him out of the pub, still screaming all the way into the car, as if she were blinded to the presence of anyone else.

'There's manners,' someone said.

'She wants one box in the jaw. Just the one,' someone else said, and there was general agreement, especially from the other women present.

But now, in her own drawing room, with no Rory, there was no sign of screaming. Aidan crossed his fingers behind his back. Perhaps he was safe. Perhaps the screaming had been reserved for Rory.

'I want to know,' she said.

It was plain that she wasn't talking about the drink she had offered him, for she had already picked up two glasses.

'About what?'

'The killing. Do they know who did it?'

'It looks like an accident, Mrs Dixon. An accident, is all.'

He didn't believe himself as he said it, but he couldn't believe either that hers was a reasonable question.

'Of course it looks like an accident,' she said. He could hear the beginnings of hysteria in her voice. She put the drink down in front of him, and he saw that her eyes were glazed over like the eyes of a dead salmon. She sat opposite, and waited for him to sit. He bent his knees and sank into the sofa, but it was too soft and low and comfortable for him to be comfortable.

'Do you smoke, Aidan?'

'I do, Mrs Dixon.'

'Can I ask you for a cigarette? I've given up, but I think I should have one now.'

He took a packet of Major from his breast pocket and offered her one. She began to look as if she were crying after the first draw.

'It was Rory who made me give up,' she said. 'We gave up together. He'd go mad if he saw me, but I suppose I can smoke as much as I want to now.'

She inhaled deeply, drawing oxygen in on top of the smoke, feeling her energy ebb as the nicotine travelled in her blood. She could see that Aidan was looking at her warily, as if she were mad and about to do something stupid. He was a very appealing young man. His ears were too big, and his face seemed about to crumple in on itself with worry, and his top and bottom teeth met at a crossed angle, which gave an impression of something infantile, of a child who hasn't quite learned how to smile yet. He thought she was mad. They all thought she was mad around here. And those who didn't thought she was stupid, but that was because she was English. That was why they always behaved like idiots in the presence of the English. They were humouring her. At least, that was what Rory had told her.

'You wouldn't have thought, would you,' she said. 'You wouldn't have thought to look at him that he was ever going to die.'

Aidan said, 'No.'

'I want to know who killed him.'

'No one killed him, Mrs Dixon.'

Then she screamed. 'How do you know? How do you bloody know? Don't patronise me.'

And then he knew, once he had been screamed at, why Rory had walked away instead of hitting her. It wasn't a scream of anger, but more like the scream of an animal as the jaws of a hound close around its throat. It was the scream of someone suffocating, and the only human thing to do was to back away so that she had space to breathe in.

He said, 'I'm sorry, Mrs Dixon.'

'No,' she said. 'It's all right. You didn't know him well enough.'

She knew that Rory didn't have accidents, and that

34

was all she knew. Someone up there liked him, and nothing had ever happened in his life that wasn't intended.

'I'd better go now, Mrs Dixon. I have to report.'

'Go,' she said. 'Go then.'

'I'm sorry for your trouble, Mrs Dixon.'

She realised that she would be hearing a lot of that little phrase over the next few weeks. They were good at death, the Irish. She realised that she didn't know the response to someone being sorry for her trouble – the niceties of death were not natural to her.

'Will you be OK on your own, Mrs Dixon? Maybe you should get a friend to come over.'

She blinked at the word friend. Her friends were Rory's friends. It was hard to think of them existing if he didn't. Then she thought of Kay. Kay was the nearest thing she had ever had to an ally.

'I'll call Kay,' she said.

As she was showing him to the door she began to cry, and said, 'Oh Jesus, I'll have to tell her. I don't want to tell her. Will you make the call for me? I'll give you the number.'

Before he left he put something in her hand, and after he was gone she saw that it was his cigarette packet. Then the grief hit her.

Friends

Beyond everything, Rory Dixon had a capacity for friendship, and once certain individuals were allowed beyond the barriers of his looks and magnetism he was the best of companions. He had a hunger to know people, to turn them upside down and see what was stamped on the base. He would ask questions that would make a psychiatric patient blush, but he got answers, because the questions were asked out of pure curiosity and out of friendship. It was a mark of this propensity that there were many who considered him to be their best friend and some who considered him to be their only friend, and with each of these individuals he gave no indication that they were less important than anyone else in his life. In the winter his life was centered on Dublin, at his offices on Eden Quay or the house in Mountpleasant Square. In the summer the focus moved to Innish, down in Wexford. Helen stayed and Rory commuted and friends came and went, many of them staying at the Commodore Hotel, which was run by Kay O'Driscoll at Cahirgavern.

Kay and her husband Jody had known the Dixons for a long time. It was through the O'Driscolls that the Dixons had discovered that part of the country and found the house at Innish. Jody was a bit of a historian who taught part-time at UCD and published small books about the Brehon Laws. Kay was the one who made the sort of money that paid for school fees and keeping up with the Dixons. She was a cynical-seeming woman with a brittle crust. If there were depths beneath that crust, and you wanted to know what they consisted of, you would have to have asked Rory. He was the only one who knew her well. And this was the Kay whom Helen nominated to be her comforter as Aidan Connelly was leaving her to her grief.

Jody and Kay were fighting as the phone went. Or, more correctly, Kay was letting fly at Jody because she said that he had been morose all afternoon. 'It's like having another bloody teenager in the house,' she said.

'Don't,' he said. He was doing his best to seem normal, so that she wouldn't ask where he had been that morning. If he could keep it up for another ten minutes she would have to go and see to her guests and the evening meal. Unfortunately they were fully staffed that week, otherwise she wouldn't have had time to notice his alleged moroseness. He kept his eyes on the papers on his desk as if he had work to do. He was making a list of the fines that were imposed for killing a man in the third century. The price of honour was graded according to the social standing of the victim, so that you could get away with the payment of a calf for killing a peasant, but you might need to pay a whole herd of cattle for killing the king. Of course you would only be killing the king if you had a chance of stepping into his shoes, so you could probably afford the fine.

He was feeling a little dizzy from looking at his lists when the phone rang. He started at the sound of it, as you would at the sound of anything you had been waiting to hear the whole evening, but at least it diverted Kay from haranguing him while she searched for the thing. 'Where's the phone? Where's the bloody phone? Why can't phones be on the end of wires any- more so you know where they are?'

He wondered whether it was pre-menstrual tension, and tried counting back the weeks to her last period. There was a time when he kept a menstrual calendar for her. It started as a joke, but in reality it was very useful. It made the whole process seem a bit more rational in some respects. He couldn't remember why he had stopped doing it, but it must have been about the time that sex between them ceased to be a recreation and became a process – the scratching of an itch for the sake of co-existence.

The phone stopped and Jack, one of their sons, came into the room holding it to his ear over the earphone of his Walkman. He was lanky and fourteen, and Jody looked at him as though he didn't quite recognise him. Things looked different all of a sudden, even his own children.

'It's for you, Mum. It's the cops.'

Kay took the phone from him with a questioning look at which he shrugged. Neither of them saw Jody's face turn stony white. By the time she had put the phone down again the contents of the call had been made plain by her part of the conversation, and Jody was rolled into a ball on the floor, pulsing and choking as though he couldn't breathe for misery. Even Jack dropped his teenage veneer of coolness and began to cry, although it wasn't clear whether he was crying for Rory, whom he had known all his life, or at the shock of seeing his father in that condition.

Kay felt idiotic as she ushered Jack from the room saying, 'Your Daddy's not well. We'd better leave him alone for a while.'

Once Jack was out of the way and she was alone with Jody, all she could feel was anger. She knelt over her husband with her hands on his shoulders, trying to coax him back into human form with gentle nonsensical words, while she really wanted to thump some sense into him. This should have been the other way around.

He had robbed her. It should have been her howling with grief and him being strong and sensible and manly. What was Rory to Jody but a friend? Given the chance, she would at that moment have told Jody of her affair with Rory, and claimed her precedence in grief as a bereaved lover. But Jody wouldn't show his face to her, and she wasn't the sort of woman who could have confessed to infidelity without looking her husband in the face. So she stroked the back of his head and said gentle words, and if she cried it was for his helplessness rather than her own loss.

'I'm going over to Helen,' she said. 'She's on her own. I might bring her back here, or I might stay the night.'

Jody seemed not to have heard.

'Will you be all right?' she asked, knowing that he wouldn't be all right, but hoping that he wouldn't be worse, and knowing that there was nothing she could do, and that if she couldn't have a moment on her own something terrible would happen. So she left him there. There were arrangements to make. Pausing by reception on her way to the kitchens, she heard herself say to the girl, 'Can you cancel the Dixons' booking for tonight. They won't be coming.' At the same time as she was proud of herself for her calmness and professionalism, she despised herself, and envied Jody his humanity.

And then she thought that she couldn't leave the boys in the house while their father was in that state, so she had to persuade them to go over to the Dillons' for the evening, and phone Mary Dillon to take them. Of course the boys objected, even though normally they pestered her to be allowed to stay at the Dillons', and said that they weren't children anymore and could look after themselves. And Dermot, who was sixteen, said, 'Of course. Get rid of us as soon as there's a crisis. That's always been the solution. Pity you could never

40

find a boarding school that was open all the summer as well.'

And she struck him in the face. She had never hit one of her children before. They had had smacks when they were little, but never a stinging slap in anger. It was the tone of his voice that made her do it. He had spoken as though he hated her. Now all three of them were looking at her with the same hate. But she didn't have time for that. She was the only one who was coping with the situation, the only one who was doing anything useful. She knew she had to be alone, and her only chance of that was the short drive from the Commodore to Innish. So she took advantage of their hatred, and while the shock was still on them she sent them down the road to the Dillons'.

She thought her own tears would come as soon as she was in the car, but anger was still all that she could feel. She sat and looked at her hotel, the big grey bald building on the edge of the sea. Before her time it had been occupied by a dwindling population of nuns, and was said to be haunted by the devil. She had always had high hopes of seeing the devil, who was supposed to be given to playing cards in what was now the ladies' lavatory. There had been a mark on the ceiling which he was said to have made, and which was said to be indelible. In the event two coats of emulsion had dealt with it, although she had had to apply them herself, since no workman in the district would risk his immortal soul. What could you do with people who believed that the devil would choose to live in a convent? She realised that she was thinking about the devil when she should be thinking about Rory, and that was when she started her car.

Something was badly wrong. Suddenly nothing was familiar, and she had to think which way to turn at every crossroads, even though at other times she could have driven the distance blindfold. And she was aware of the space between her two arms as they held the steering wheel, until she could almost feel Rory's torso filling the space, and smell him as though he were sleeping in her arms. So by the time she had stopped the car outside the house at Innish she had almost erased the happenings of the last hour from her mind, and no longer believed that Rory was dead, but that he would open the door to her and everything would be as usual, with he and she and Helen talking over supper, he and she careful not to give even a knowing smile to each other while Helen was in the room, showing no sign that either of them was remembering their last assignation or contemplating their next.

She found Helen in the kitchen, hunched over the table, her form outlined against the window and the shimmering gloom of a dull summer evening. And she couldn't help thinking that Helen had always been given to sulking in the dark when left to her own devices. This was not the first time she had found her in that attitude. Kay switched on the light for want of something to say.

Helen's face was a void. There was a glass in her hand and an empty green cigarette packet beside her. She had smoked all of Aidan Connelly's cigarettes, one after another, until her throat ached and the smell from the ashtray gave her nausea. She made no sign of noticing Kay, or that the light had been turned on.

Kay said, 'Can I do anything for you?'

Helen started, and looked in the direction of Kay's voice.

'It's only me,' Kay said. 'Have you eaten?'

'No,' Helen said. 'No, I couldn't.'

Helen's eyes had a damned look in them, as though she couldn't focus on anything in the material world. When Kay saw that, she knew that Helen's loss had been greater than her own. Rory had been a lover and a source of happiness for Kay, but he had been pivotal to the whole of Helen's life – the focus of love and hatred and everything in between. And once she had realised that, Kay could go and take the widow's hand and give her sympathy.

Helen said, 'They are going to treat it as an accident. They won't do anything about finding out who did it.'

Kay stroked the diamonds and the bones of the widow's fingers and said, 'I'm sure they know how to go about these things. If they say it was an accident, then it must be true.'

Helen said, 'They haven't decided anything yet. But I know that is what they are going to do. There are interests to be served. McGrath and Foley and the rest of them are up to their necks in it.'

'Up to their necks in what?'

'I don't know. Yet.'

'So what makes you think so?' Kay regretted having asked that question, because Helen seemed too weary to answer it, and then Helen looked at her as if the question had been idiotic, and rallied herself.

'Well, what would you think?' she said. Her voice was reasoned, but implausible in the circumstances, because widows of a few hours, particularly those of Helen's temperament, are not expected to be rational. 'Do you think that Rory was given every major contract in Dublin for the last ten years because his buildings are nicer than anyone else's? Do you think we have people like Andy McGrath to supper for the pleasure of his company? Do you?'

Kay didn't know what to answer. Andy McGrath, who was now the Local Government Minister in the coalition government, although not the most person-able of God's creatures, was Rory's oldest friend. Indeed, she even knew the story, from pillow talk with Rory, of the night of Rory and Helen's meeting and the two single beds in the Shelbourne Hotel. She knew that Helen would have objections to Andy McGrath's

43

company that had nothing to do with the fact that he held his knife like a pencil.

Kay said, 'I don't know what to think. I don't know if you're being serious. I don't even know if it matters whether it was an accident or not. I don't know if I believe that Rory is dead.'

Helen said, 'I never doubted it. I knew as soon as Aidan Connelly said it that it was true. If you knew Rory as I did, you would know that his death would be a lie beyond the human imagination.'

'I knew him well enough,' Kay said that in irritation, hoping afterwards that the irritation hadn't been evident, and fearing the worst on hearing what Helen said next.

'Do you think that Rory was faithful to me?'

'Yes,' Kay said. 'I don't know. I think he loved you. I think it comes to the same thing.'

Helen said, 'Does it?' But in spite of that she seemed comforted by what Kay had said. She smiled. 'I even thought once that he was having an affair with you.'

'Did you?'

'Not for long. There were two things that changed my mind. One was seeing you put your hand on Jody's one day, and there was real tenderness, and then I knew that you weren't capable of it.'

'And the other?'

'Seeing Rory and Jody together, and knowing that he wouldn't do that to his friend. They were too close.'

'Jody's taking it badly. Worse than any of us.' Kay was desperate for the change of subject. She felt more than the awkwardness of dissimulation; she felt dirty talking to Helen about Rory as if she were Helen's friend, as if they were united against him. For years and years she had sat through Helen's tirades against Rory: how the man was destroying her; lists of suspicions and accusations; denigration of his personal habits, of things which should not be accounted for outside a marriage. While he had been alive it was bearable, because it was like a joke, and while she sympathised with Helen and nodded her head and tutted, Kay would be summoning up details of his body in her mind, enjoying the duplicity of confidence and betrayal. Now that he was dead it was different, and Rory was the only one being betrayed, and she had a hard time not telling Helen that she had never deserved the man.

'Poor Jody,' was all Helen said.

And that, thought Kay, was Helen. She could never have more than a token of empathy for anyone other than herself.

Kay thought of something. 'Have you told Corinna?'

Helen looked surprised. 'Do you think she'd want to know?'

'Sweet Jesus. She's his daughter. Do you have her number? I'll phone her now.'

'No,' Helen said. 'Can't we leave it until the morning? Hell is going to break loose in the morning anyway. Can't we leave everything until then? Corinna doesn't give a damn about her father.'

These people are shadows from this distance, and their thoughts are shadows of shadows. Kay, thinking of the line of hair that ran from his navel, thinking of his navel, desperate to see his body once again, but knowing that it would not be enough to see it as a mourner would. She would want to see his body in its entirety; she would want to see tumescence. And in grief these shadows of people lost their character because, although their loss was expressed in different ways, it was all one grief. And for once I had some inkling of what they felt. Though still divorced from them by deity, I too was at a loss, and at a worse loss than those who had known what it was to lie in his arms. When Kay O'Driscoll thought of a line of hair on his body,

45

she could remember her own finger running along that line of hair. She could remember moments of feeling that she was not entirely alone in the universe. She spent the evening with Helen, wife and mistress in the stainless steel kitchen, each becoming like the other in their sorrow and in the things they couldn't say to one another. I began to feel excluded, and I turned my attention elsewhere.

Family

Denny Power looked like Rasputin, and probably didn't smell very different if you got close to him. Most of the general public were spared that fate by the width of a bar counter, and by the smoke-thickened atmosphere of his pub. It was where a lot of the younger people of Gavinstown went to drink, and smoke a bit of dope if they could get any, where intense conversations were held despite the deafening thrash and grunge music and the space between the ears of most of the clientship. At closing time the shutters were put up and the music was turned down a little and the crowd thinned marginally, but the drinking went on. On the few occasions when Denny Power's had been raided it was remarked that none of his friends or regulars had been on the premises, only a few hapless teenagers who could be sacrificed to the moral indignation of the town and the myth of police incorruptibility. Denny Power himself had become a bit of a legend, with his string of battered women and malnourished children, and the allegations and rumours that he was involved in everything from soft drugs to white slavery. Although it was hardly conceivable that he had a hand in everything he was accused of, his reputation was good for business and attracted every Doc Martin-shod small town rebel from a ten mile radius on any night of the week that they weren't slam-dancing in Waterford.

It was while drinking in Denny Power's that Corinna Dixon heard of the death of her father. By coincidence she heard it from Alan Kehoe, not many hours after he had brought the body back to Ballinglass. It was Alan's first time in Denny's and he was without his girlfriend. They had fought and parted an hour before in Mangan's disco because he was being, in her opinion, more amorous than the occasion demanded. Feeling reckless, he strayed into Denny's. Apart from anything else, he knew that his presence in a place like that would be something to throw in his mother's face in the morning, if he condescended to speak to her again.

Once inside the door he felt a bit lost and out of his depth, as though he were being scrutinised covertly by Denny and the hard chaws at the bar. But he thought that ordering a drink was preferable to scuttling out again as if he had been intimidated by the place. It was like someone's vision of hell, packed with greasy hair and black leather and smoke, with the music so loud that you felt it would be an effort to walk through the noise. There was only one face that he recognised, and although it was someone he had never particularly liked, any kind of familiarity in that place was welcome to him. He went over to say hello, and sat down at the same table, and after a while found himself in conversation with the girl on his left, who was Corinna Dixon.

For some reason or other, he found Corinna attractive and imagined her to be sympathetic, despite her appearance. Her head was shaven at the temples and she wore a stud in her nose and leather thongs around her neck, but she seemed to be pleasant and relaxed. He didn't know that she was stoned out of her box, and he could barely make out anything that she said above the noise of the music, although she seemed to understand every word of his, being used to conversation under such circumstances. By the time he was on his third pint he felt that he could trust her, and began to tell her about his adventures earlier in the day, and she listened as if he was telling a good story, until he told her the name of the man whose corpse he had retrieved. And then she seemed a bit odd, and he asked her if she had known the man, and she said that she had, and got up to leave.

He swallowed the last three-quarters of his pint and followed her, as much because he didn't want to be left on his own in Denny's as because he wanted to go after her. He caught up with her at the door and they walked along the street together, she taking no notice of his presence until he asked her where they were going.

'I don't know where you're going,' she said. 'I know where I'm going.'

It might have been the drink, but he loved her voice: too rich to be a girl's, not deep enough to be a boy's; like the voice of an older woman who has smoked forty a day all her life. He regretted the hour he had wasted not being able to hear it in the pub.

'How did you know Rory Dixon?' he said. He asked it as much to hear her voice as out of curiosity. He was feeling unusually euphoric now that he was out in the fresh air, but made no connection between that and the effect of the atmosphere in Denny's on his virgin lungs.

'He used to be my father,' she said.

That killed off the smalltalk for a few hundred yards and then, for want of words that would ease him out of his embarrassment, he put his arm across her shoulders, and she carried on walking as if she hadn't noticed.

They had left Gavinstown and were walking upriver, along the Dublin road, when they passed the track that led down to the burn-out ruins of the Riverside Lodge Hotel. They both took this track without spoken agreement or hesitation, stumbling a little where it was dark

49

and overhung by trees. Once they were in the grounds of the hotel they could see quite clearly, by the light of the stars and the reflection from the river and the glow of streetlamps from the town. They sat side by side on a stone wall over the glistening tidal mud.

'I'm sorry about your father,' he said.

'I'm not,' she said.

'Oh,' he said.

It was only then that it occurred to him to wonder why they had come here and the idea of physical intimacy began to form in his brain, and then his groin. He wondered if it was fate or what, and whether what he had felt with her father's dead body in the water was only a premonition of what he hoped would happen now. He knew he had to make a move at that moment, or doubt his own sexuality forever. He slid his arm back over her shoulders and put his lips against the side of her neck.

She stood up, but without drawing away, and he stood up to match her, without being ready for what she did next. She put her hand down the front of his trousers and held his erection, as if it were the handlebar of a bicycle. He was a bit shocked, because they hadn't even kissed yet, and he had assumed that these things were supposed to be taken in stages, not that he had any previous experience to refer to. He assumed that the favour was to be returned, and made the appropriate gesture – timidly enough, fortunately, for it to be well received.

They did it lying on a narrow stone wall, and it was over in a few bewildering moments. He was too worried about falling into the river mud to take any pleasure from it, or even to be sure that he was inside her at all, but assumed afterwards that he had been, because of the soreness.

She slipped away without any more being said. Modestly he had gone into the shadows to relieve himself,

50

and when he returned she was gone. He stayed there by the river until the small hours of the morning, remembering and memorizing every moment of it: the squeak of her leather jacket; the thud of her heavy boots against the side of the wall; the acrid smell of her breath; the scoring of her fingernail in his arsehole; the feint, token way she kissed him afterwards as she wiped herself with his shirt-tail. He tore off that part of his shirt and held it to his nose for a long time, even though it smelled mostly of himself, and before he went home he rolled it into a ball and canted it far out into the river. Never spill your seed upon the ground.

Corinna had gone straight home, feeling nothing. She climbed the hill to the council estate and let herself in by the back door. David was waiting up for her, with the baby asleep across his knee. She waited for him to ask her where she had been, even though he would know she had been to Denny Power's.

Instead he just said, 'Your father's dead.'

'I know,' she said.

He looked down at the baby across his knee. 'I fed him an hour ago,' he said, and then added unnecessarily, 'He's asleep now.'

She said, 'Thanks,' and took the baby up without waking him and carried him upstairs. When David had turned off the lights and the television and followed, he found them both in bed, she curled around the sleeping child, crying.

'Do you want me in here tonight?' He spoke apologetically, trying to keep the tremble out of his voice, knowing that she didn't like his eagerness to be near her.

'Yes,' she said, without looking at him.

He went to the other room to get his alarm clock, and then to the bathroom to undress, peeing against the side of the bowl for silence, ashamed of the noise of the lavatory when it flushed. When he came back to her she had put the baby in his cot and was lying again in the same position, but not crying anymore. He got into the bed as though she were asleep and he were afraid of waking her, and gradually insinuated his soft furry body against hers until he was making love to her.

That night she kept him awake with her dreams more than usual, jabbering and crying into the pillow. At six the alarm went, without waking her. He got up to change and feed the baby before going to work. When he left at a quarter to seven, they were both snoring peacefully. He would have liked to kiss his sleeping wife goodbye before leaving, but he thought it might be better to leave things as they were, just in case.

David and Corinna had been married less than a year. The baby was four months old and was his, as far as either of them could guess, though he was perfectly aware that it might not be so. They had gone to England to marry in a registry office, at her insistence and to the disappointment of his family, if they could have been more disappointed than they were at his marrying her at all. She had named the baby Sid, because it was a name she liked. But she told people that it was after Sid Vicious, because she knew it was a cause of annoyance. She insisted that she would still be called Corinna Dixon, and wouldn't answer to anyone who called her Mrs Kennedy. She was nineteen years of age, though she could look younger. He was twenty-three.

After washing the mug from which he had drunk his tea, after closing the back door softly, he negotiated the junk that littered the small yard he hadn't yet had time to clear and propped the falling gate shut behind him. When they married, Rory and Helen had offered to buy them a house, but Corinna had refused and put her name on the housing list while they prepared for a long wait in his parents' back bedroom. But Rory must have pulled some political strings or something, because they were given the next council house that became vacant. The housing scheme was a new one, which was unfortunate, because cheap materials and some highbrow architect's idea of modernity made the houses practically uninhabitable.

While he worked during the day, she and the baby watched television. In the evening he cooked for them, usually a fry. Although she sometimes said that she was a vegetarian, she didn't seem to notice what she ate. As far as he could tell, she seemed to have gotten over the anorexia business since her pregnancy. He thought she was still too thin, but never said anything about it. She might be vomiting still, even though there was no sign of it evident to him. Three or four nights a week she went out on her own, almost always to Denny Power's. She had never asked his permission, and he had never tried to stop her. If he was still up when she came in he would ask her where she had been, in a tone of friendly enquiry with no hint of accusation. She always gave Denny's as her answer and he left it at that.

He knew that she slept around, but was too much in love with her to protest and tried not to think about it. When he did think about it he cried his guts out. On the other hand, when she returned and he thought she had been with someone else, he found himself extraordinarily aroused. He knew the nights when she had been with someone else because those were the nights when he didn't have to sleep in the other room, the nights she let him make love to her. Do what he might to stop it, he always imagined her with other men while they were fucking. It wasn't fantasy and it wasn't nightmare, but somewhere between the two. It was himself he hated for this, as though he were the unfaithful one. He never resented her for what he saw as his failing, because he loved her too much.

He had to be in the post office yard by seven to load his van before beginning the round. He never had much to say to the other men, not knowing how much they knew about his marriage through small town gossip, nor knowing which, if any of them, had slept with his wife. He couldn't help speculating about that and would often find himself staring at the crotches of other men, wondering, and despising himself for it. Through all of this he never regretted his marriage to Corinna, and considered himself lucky to know her at all. It wasn't, he told himself, her fault.

Once he had started the engine and was heading downriver towards the first house on his round there was a kind of relief. The beginning of work meant that he had to think about other things, and all the people he would meet during the day were country people, people he had no reason to think knew anything about him. With one terrible exception: Innish was on his round. Every working day he had to handle letters with Rory Dixon's name on them. Not for much longer, he thought, now that the man was dead.

Helen was waiting for him outside the front door of Innish. She looked as though she had lost her marbles. Her hair was unbrushed and her shirt would have looked as if she had slept in it, if she had looked as if she had slept. He rolled down his window to hand her the letters.

'Rory's dead,' she said.

'I know. I heard about it last night.' He could hear the resentment in his voice, and was pleased to hear it. He and Corinna should have been told. He shouldn't have had to hear about the death of his father-in-law from his next door neighbour, who had heard it down the street in Gavinstown. He was holding out the letters to Helen, but she was showing no sign of taking them. She was staring at him like a madwoman, or like his idea of a madwoman, which was only based on his experience of her.

'Does Corinna know?' she asked.

'No thanks to you,' he said, and having said it his bitterness went into remission for a moment and the habit of good manners prevailed. 'I'm sorry for your trouble, Mrs Dixon. It was a terrible accident.' He called her Mrs Dixon because she had never invited him to do otherwise.

'It wasn't an accident,' she said. 'He was murdered.' She said it in such a straightforward way that he thought for two seconds that it must be official, and the colour drained from his face. Then she said, 'No one will believe me. But I know.'

Then he knew that it was only her own warped imagination. He was saved from having to think of something else to say by the sound of another car drawing up behind him. He pushed the letters towards her with one hand while putting the car into gear with the other. This time she took the letters and he could drive away. It wasn't only on Corinna's behalf that he hated her. She had always looked down on him, not with overt snobbery, because her sort were too politically correct for that, but she belittled him on intellectual grounds, using words that she knew he wouldn't understand, asking questions about his family and background that were supposed to sound concerned but which, in fact, were designed to expose his putative inferiority and lack of worth. But it would seem now that she had finally flipped, and he was glad. He had enjoyed seeing her without her armour of barbed remarks and he liked the idea of her being dragged off by men in white coats.

Three times he said, 'Stupid mad English snobby bitch' as he returned along the drive, between the horse chestnut trees where he had had his first sighting of Corinna, a long time before he met her.

He wondered if he shouldn't have taken the day off to be with Corinna. It hadn't occurred to him before, because when she wanted him to do something she would usually ask. He thought that the best he could do now was to get his round over as quickly as possible, and return to her. The day was turning out to be a hot one. As he passed the turning for Craggin Strand he decided that if he could finish early enough he might borrow his brother's car and take Corinna and Sid for a swim. Sid hadn't been to the beach yet. He drove along, planning the hot late afternoon on the sand, and the van picked up speed down the hill of the headland, towards the turn above the Black Rock.

It was hard to watch. Not that I would have given a hoot if David Kennedy went over the cliff, but it reminded me of the day before, and instead of the green post office van I saw the blue Spider. I had to stop watching for a moment. There was a time when I couldn't do that, when I thought it was my duty to watch and guide every moment of human existence. And look where that got me. Got you. And then guidance went out of the window, a long time ago by your standards. And then there was only watching the masturbating, defecating, self-satisfied horde of you. Not that I have any basic objections to any of those, human, traits, although given the choice I'd rather watch you wank than shit. For the first time in my life, as the green van shot down the hill, I stopped watching, but only for the most token of moments.

There was activity on the cliffs that day. There was a lifting machine and a squad car and men with cameras. If he hadn't been thinking about Corinna on the sand, David would have wondered what they were doing there. It wasn't until later in the day that he put two and two together.

The Minister

It was Andy McGrath who was disgorged from the vehicle which drew up behind David Kennedy's van at Innish that morning. The same Andy McGrath who had been Rory's conspirator in lust in their youth, who had slept with Helen on the night she met Rory, who had served as best man on the day of their wedding and godfather to Corinna on what had laughably been called her christening. Laughable because not one of the people in the church that day had the smallest shred of faith in me, let alone in the cult of Christ. Even the priest, after years of doubt, had come to the conclusion that it was the here and now that mattered. Within weeks of baptising Corinna he was to abscond to Manchester with the parish funds and his house-keeper's daughter.

In those days Andy was an overweight young solicitor and a bit of a rake. It was at Corinna's christening party, having wet the baby's head a little too freely, that he and Rory embarked upon a political argument, the result of which was that Rory bet him a hundred pounds that he couldn't get himself elected to local government. Andy remembered the bet and Rory lost it. By recognising opportunities, in time Andy clawed his way through the ranks and scandals to become a minister of, ironically enough, Local Government. That he looked like a politician may have been on his side.

He was corpulent enough to satisfy the Shakespearean Caesar's criterion of trustworthiness, without being so fat as to seem gluttonous and complacent; he was ugly enough not to threaten the male voter and oily enough to reassure the female. He was possessed of a wife who wore fake Chanel, and three seemingly well-adjusted children, none of whom objected to smiling at cameras. He never expressed an opinion whose origins could be traced back to himself, and his response to a question was never the answer to the question itself. Most of those who knew him well in a personal capacity disliked him intensely. But those who knew him slightly or not at all found him charming and reassuring, since above all he exuded an impression of reliability and competence.

His long-standing friendship with Rory mystified some. On the surface the two had little in common. Even those who saw failings in Rory could see that he was genuine, while Andy's greatest supporters would have to admit in private that the minister was false. But the provenance of the friendship was the bonds of hedonism, and over the years neither had lost his taste for pleasure, though each of them was forced to disguise it to some degree except from each other, until they were tied to one another by confidences and secrets and the knowledge that they each had someone to whom they could expose their entire disgusting selves without fear of recrimination. And then they came to the stage in life when your oldest friends are the easiest to be with, when even though they may have the sort of faults which would be grounds for rejection in a new acquaintance these faults can be ignored through familiarity: because the presence of a friend is comforting, and there are moments when presence is all that is required, times when you don't want to have to justify yourself as you would with a lover or a stranger.

Once out of his car, Andy McGrath smoothed the

lariat of hair which curled over the bald portion of his head and walked towards the widow with open arms.

'Helen,' he said. 'I'm sorry for your trouble.' His voice was unctuous perhaps, but that may have been force of habit. He had the look of a man who had spent a troubled night, and we should allow ourselves to think that the death of Rory Dixon had a traumatic effect even on such a creature as he.

For an answer, or maybe to avoid an embrace, Helen handed him the letters she was carrying and walked into the house. He understood by his possession of the letters that he was to follow her. She was standing in the hall, holding a staring match with the glass eyes of a dead fox.

'I know why you're here,' she said.

He put the letters down on the long oak table that ran the length of the hall. It was on this table that the coats of guests were piled during parties. He couldn't see there would be any more of these parties now that Rory was gone. No one in their right mind would come all the way out here just to see Helen.

'I only came out to see you,' he said. 'To see if there was anything I could do for you.'

'There's quite a lot you could do for me,' she said. 'But if we are going to talk about what you will do for me, it might be a short conversation.'

'I'll do anything I can,' he said.

She disengaged her eyes from the fox's mask and looked at him.

'I need a drink,' he said and, without waiting for her to offer him one, walked into the drawing room.

'You know where it is,' she said in a sarcastic tone, not loud enough for him to have heard. She knew she would have to speak to him, to get him on her side. In the troubles to come he could be her strongest ally, if he were willing to help her at all. For the moment she should repress her distaste of him. She forced herself to walk through the drawing room door in his wake.

He was standing by the window with a glass of whisky in his hand. He nodded towards the avenue of horse chestnuts.

'Rory was going to plant a second lot in between them,' he said. 'So they'd be mature when the old trees had to come down.'

'Rory was going to do a lot of things,' she said.

'Maybe you should go ahead with it. As a memorial. Each of his friends could plant a tree for him.'

She was going to say something sharp about it being a good photo-opportunity for a politician, but she remembered that she had to be sweet to him so said, 'Maybe.'

'A tragedy,' he said. 'A terrible accident.'

He was watching her to see what she would say, but she was on her guard. She knew why he had come and she wasn't going to let him accomplish his mission as easily as that. She said nothing, forcing him to go further.

'I hear,' he said, 'that you have your suspicions about it.'

'Who told you that?' She found herself speaking casually, with an unfounded confidence that she could beat him at his own game.

'Ah,' he said, 'I heard. These things get around.'

'Foley?'

'Have you spoken to Foley?'

'You know I haven't,' she said. 'But you have. So what did he tell you?'

'He thought you might be a bit upset.'

'I knew it,' she said. 'I knew that was why you came. Foley tipped you off that I was on to something and you came rushing over here to persuade me that I'm off my rocker.'

'No,' he said. 'Helen. Look.'

'Helen look yourself. I know. I knew Rory. If anyone

60

wants me to think it was an accident then they are
going to have to prove it. And even if it is proved, it
will only be a cover-up.' She knew she had lost it now.
She had lost control of her voice, and lost control of
the conversation. She tried to draw herself back, to
seem less as though she were ranting, but she could
hear her voice carry on as if it had a mind of its own.
'This is what my life with that man consisted of. Things
are hidden from me. It's like being haunted, and whenever you say that you've seen something people look
at you as though you are mad.'

He said, 'So what have you seen?'

She said, 'I've seen you come haring over here in a
panic. That speaks for itself. Shouldn't you be running
a government department, or flying off to Brussels or
something?'

He looked out across the grass towards the sea,
where the air was already beginning to shake and crack
with the heat of the sun. 'Rory was my best friend,' he
said. 'That's why I'm here.'

For a moment she almost believed him, and said,
'Then get them to find out who killed him.'

He took her arm and led her to a sofa so that she
could sit down. It wasn't until his hand was beneath
her elbow that she realised she had been shaking. He
squatted before her on his hunkers, with his right arm
stretched out and his great ham of a hand resting on
her shoulder. He knew the tricks of intimacy from his
election campaigns. There were ways of touching
people without compromising them, ways of forcing
them into your confidence. He looked directly into her
eyes as if she were a camera lens.

'Helen, look. At some point this morning the newspapers are going to turn up here. They're down at the
Black Rock already. I'm not saying it wasn't an accident
and I'm not saying it was. There's nothing known yet.
But if Rory was killed I'll be the first to want to know

61

who and why. And the way you're talking won't help things. People will think that you are being hysterical and that can only hinder the chances of an investigation. I'm going to do what I can to help, and in the meantime you can help by not talking to the papers.'

'Can I trust you?' she said. She knew that she couldn't trust him, but in part she was hypnotised by him, and in part she was convinced by him that it might be in her best interests to agree with him.

'Of course,' he said. 'Look, I suggest you go back to Dublin for now. There isn't anything you can do here.'

'I'm going to stay at the Commodore,' she said. 'Kay offered to put me up for a few nights, just until the funeral.'

'Good girl. Is he going to be buried here, or in Dublin?'

'Here,' she said. 'Right here. I want him to be buried at Innish.'

'You might need planning permission for that.'

'Well?' she said.

'What are friends for?' he said. 'I'll fix it.'

She said, 'Thank you,' but in a way that was oddly formal, and in contrast to his over-friendly tones.

'Have you thought what you might do?' he said.

'Do?'

'I suppose it's a bit soon. You can't have had time to think about it yet. Do you think you'll stay in Ireland?'

'Stay in Ireland?' she said.

Her concentration was gone. He wondered if she was taking something to sedate her, but it was really only exhaustion. She had spent the night pacing the rooms of the house. She wasn't capable of thinking what country she would live in, or whom she could go to. She had no family of her own that she knew of. Not since her sister had died. She began thinking that everyone she would have turned to was dead, and wondering if death wasn't the only place left for her. She began

62

to feel another wash of sadness creep towards her, and she would have to stem it while Andy was there. Until he was gone sadness could be weakness and weakness would be danger.

'I'd kill for a cigarette,' she said.

He only just checked himself from saying that Rory wouldn't like to hear her say that.

'Would you now,' he said. 'Have you eaten?'

'Why does everyone ask that? My husband has just been murdered, and all anyone can ask is whether I've eaten. Well, I haven't eaten, and I'm not going to eat. I don't see myself as the fat widow.'

Andy smiled at her indulgently. It was one of a range of smiles he had for television, so it looked slightly odd in life, or in profile. Luckily, she wasn't looking at him but down at her own stomach, criticising its miniscule convexity with a hardened dieter's eyes. Then she got up and wandered out of the room and out of the house, and he watched her make towards the sea like a sleepwalker.

As soon as she was out of earshot he picked up the phone and called Kay to make sure it was true that Helen was going to stay at the Commodore.

'And there'll be the papers,' he said. 'If they find out where she is, try to keep them away from her. And if she goes on about this murder business, don't contradict her. You'll only make her worse. It'll all blow over once he's buried, and maybe then we can get her a bit of professional help.'

Having no reason to believe that he wasn't speaking in Helen's best interests, Kay agreed with him, and they discussed more practical arrangements, such as getting word to Rory's parents in Manantavaddi, and dealing with Corinna and the solicitors and the undertakers. Andy said he would look in at Rory's offices in Eden Quay that afternoon to see what needed to be done there.

63

'It's just as well he had friends,' he said. 'She isn't in the best of form.'

When he had finished on the telephone, he went to take his leave of her. He saw her in the distance. She was down on the small private beach below the house, striking a dramatic pose in front of the sea. He decided not to disturb her, half hoping, if the truth were known, that she might walk into the sea and drown herself. That would tie up an awful lot of loose ends. The only drawback he could think of was that it might be bad publicity for him to have been the last person to see her alive.

Seeing

Omnipresence is not a problem. You get used to seeing everything all at once, and for centuries the novelty of it is exciting. But in old age you narrow your focus; you specialise; you look for small metaphoric incidents when you are feeling conscientious. More often you are only looking for a bit of excitement. From this distance the most profound human moments can be no more than titillation, the world I am said to have created no more than a docudrama. If you think that the Nine O'Clock News has given you compassion fatigue, then think what these millenia of viewing have done for me. Omnipresence seemed a wonderful idea when there was wonderful idealism, but now it seems more like the voyeurism of an old God: the image of man, but trapped in an existence where there is no goddess whose buttocks I can curl around at night; no night; no catamite whose tense body I can call up in my memory when solitude turns to loneliness. So I watch, folded about myself with longing.

And there it all is. Never mind the famines and the wars and the camps and the caviare-fed dictators shitting on humanity. Never mind the rainforests and the ozone layer and the rivers of black chemical sludge. Just take one small country: a modern democratic republic with a relatively wealthy and highly-educated population, sufficiently homogeneous to be capable of avoiding racial or sectarian hatred (we are talking about the republic now, not the island as a whole), and watch the things that are done, in private, often in my name. There is the woman in County Clare who has never touched her own nipples in forty years of adult life for fear of offending me. If you could understand that woman you could extrapolate a formula which might explain the rest of it. If you could watch that woman you might be tempted to keep that tenner you sent to Bob Geldof and buy yourself the makings of a couple of fat joints. You'd be amazed what people get up to. Then again, you probably do worse yourself, but you won't admit it. Andy McGrath pisses in the sink while he brushes his teeth, to save time in the mornings. Sergeant Foley masturbates into a pair of women's shoes which he keeps in a locked cupboard expressly for that purpose. Kay O'Driscoll can bring herself to orgasm by squeezing her thighs together on crowded trains.

Alan Kehoe began to hang around in Denny Power's on any night of the week he could get a lift into Gavinstown, hoping desperately to meet Corinna again. He asked cautious questions about her, so cautious that it took him three nights to find out that she was married and a mother, and another night to find out where she lived. He would prowl over the council estate in the early hours, watching the windows of her house until dawn, when he would go down to the main road and stick his thumb out for a lift back to Ballinglass. He was beyond the point where anyone could talk to him and beyond caring what his mother got up to with Moby. Out in the boat he worked automatically, hardly speaking or acknowledging Moby's existence. He was losing weight and acquiring an ugly turn to his mouth.

Because of the difficulty in getting word to Rory's parents in Manantavaddi, and the red tape to be cleared away for a burial on private ground, it was eight days before the funeral could take place. Helen didn't go to stay at the Commodore in the end. She changed her mind when Kay came to fetch her, saying that she was unable to go beyond the gate until matters were settled. She spent the days haunting the house and garden, without changing her clothes or washing. Kay brought her food, and after the third day she began to eat a little, in a distracted manner. She went on and on about the murder, and Kay had to listen to far-fetched theories about who could have done it and why. The strain was showing on Kay. She still had a hotel to run and it was the height of the season, and Jody had become impossible, a shell of grief, mourning his dead friend with an intensity that no one could understand. He never spoke now or answered her, but sat at his desk all day with his head in his hands and, when she was finally driven to shouting at him, locked himself in a bathroom for hours. She sent the three boys off to their grandparents' for a holiday, but that brought no relief, only guilt.

The coroner's verdict was accidental death by drowning. Andy called in a few favours and kept the press away from Helen, and it looked as though the whole thing would pass over as nothing more than a tragedy. Then on the fifth day, Helen was moping in Rory's workroom and, more in idleness than anything, began to press the buttons on his answering machine. There was a time when she used to listen to his messages to try to prove his infidelity, but not often, since it was unlikely that a secret lover would be stupid enough to leave that sort of evidence. She listened to them now as a form of self-torture. They all predated his death: calls from the office mostly. There was a slightly frantic call from Jody. Poor Jody was always getting worked up about something or other. He must have been more dependent on Rory than she had realised.

Then, just as the self-torture was taking effect and

she was becoming weepy, there was a message from a strange voice, one which gave no name and was so muffled that you could hardly tell if it was a man or a woman. She had to rewind it and play it several times to understand it completely.

It said, 'You've had the friendly warnings, Dixon. This is just to let you know that your time is up. I'm sure you know what the consequences are. Say a prayer, Dixon.'

It was a threat, but to her it was evidently a death threat. She phoned the barracks, but couldn't be coherent enough to make the man on the desk understand what she wanted. In the end he put her through to Aidan Connelly, and Aidan left a word for the sergeant and came straight round to Innish.

By the time he got there she was calm again, and triumphant. She somehow imagined that she had broken through the wall that was between her and the rest of the world. She greeted Aidan with what she took to be dignified righteousness. But all he saw was a dirty, dishevelled and emaciated woman with a mad glint in her eye and a cassette tape in her right hand. She brought him to the workroom and put the tape in the machine, and he listened to the distorted voice.

'Well?' she said.

'Well now,' he said.

'Well, do something,' she said. 'It's the proof. You have no choice now. Someone murdered Rory and his voice is on the machine.'

'Things would seem to be pointing that way,' he said.

He was in a bind. The tape confirmed suspicions that he already had, deeply repressed because they were based on nothing more than instinct and because his position wasn't powerful enough for his instincts to count for anything, but mostly because his instinct was in direct conflict with the case the sergeant had taken so much trouble to make.

'I didn't catch it all,' he said.

She rewound the tape and was about to play it again when the doorbell rang.

'Shouldn't you answer that?' he said.

'Not now. Just listen.'

He was listening when the sergeant, who had found the door open and only rung the doorbell as a token, came into the room, and said, 'Well, now, what's all this in aid of?'

Aidan and Helen started, as if they had been caught in a delicate position, and if Aidan was embarrassed afterwards it was because he had started when he had no reason to. He often thought later that a lot of subsequent trouble would have been saved if he had reacted normally when the sergeant made his entrance, if he hadn't been too abashed to stand up to him when the sergeant began bullying Helen.

She recovered herself more quickly. 'Good,' she said. 'It was you I wanted to hear this. There's no way out of a murder investigation now.'

The sergeant listened twice and was halfway through the second playing when he said, 'What proof is that of anything? You can only make out one word in three.'

That was when Aidan should have interposed, but he only sat in the background, red-faced.

Helen said, 'I knew you'd say that. I've written it down. I've typed it in case you suddenly found you couldn't read my handwriting.' She couldn't help the sarcasm, even though she knew that antagonising Foley would get her nowhere.

Foley read the piece of paper she handed him, sighing as if he were dealing with a stupid child and forcing himself to be patient, and said, 'This proves nothing. I'm sorry, Mrs Dixon, but the death was an accident. It would take more than this to overturn a coroner's verdict. It could be a joke. Your husband had friends who were fond of a joke, Mrs Dixon. And if you don't mind me saying so, I know things are hard for you at the moment, but the Gardai have serious work to be getting on with without having to deal with jokes.'

She felt the bile rise in her and she glared at him, making herself look even more unhinged. 'The car,' she said. 'What about the car? Was the car examined?'

'Of course we examined it,' he said.

'And?' she said.

'And we found nothing that suggested anything other than an accident. The man was driving too fast and he missed a bend in the road.'

'You're lying,' she said.

'That's a very serious allegation, Mrs Dixon. In front of a witness.'

They both looked at Aidan, and Aidan looked at his boots. He knew now that something was going on. If it was true that Helen was only a harmless hysteric, driven out of her mind by the death, then the sergeant would be treating her with more consideration. His face went red again, but with frustration in place of embarrassment.

She was addressing the sergeant again. You couldn't help noticing that there was something stagey about her voice, like a bad actress playing a rôle out of her depth. 'You know as well as I do that that car was like a chemist's shop on wheels. Are you saying that when you examined the car you failed to notice his stash of dope in the glove compartment, or the coke behind the ashtray?'

Foley began speaking to her between his teeth, as if menace would succeed where condescension had failed. 'We found no illegal substances on the vehicle or on the body, Mrs Dixon. If however you are suggesting to me that these substances exist, we would have to conclude that they were on these premises and if we were to find them, you, as the sole occupant, would be held liable. I'd hate to see you saddled with a prison sentence on top of your other troubles, Mrs Dixon.'

He had her in a corner. For the moment she was defeated. In the background she could hear the answering machine rewind itself, and then the bleeps.

'Well, Mrs Dixon?' he said.

She wouldn't answer him, so he said, 'If you have any more problems, Mrs Dixon, I suggest you get in touch with your doctor, and leave us to get on with our job.'

She had turned her head away from them, indicating perhaps that they should see themselves out. Foley put his hand on the answering machine and said, 'I'll be taking the tape with me, in case it's needed.'

She grabbed the machine from beneath his hand, took it away and shouted, 'No. If you want it badly enough you'll have to get one of your bloody warrants.'

'In that case we'll be saying good day to you, Mrs Dixon.'

He nodded to Aidan and left the room. Aidan would have liked to hang back for a second, just long enough to tell her that he was sorry and that he would do what he could. But he couldn't trust her to be discreet and was afraid of compromising himself. He shuffled away after the sergeant without even trying to catch her eye.

It was when they had gone that she realised to what extent she was on her own. She felt that she had been idiotic to go along with Andy McGrath. It was plain to her now that he and Foley were in it together. Not that that necessarily made either one of them Rory's killer. It could just be that they had something else to hide which a general investigation would uncover.

Through the frustration of knowing these things came a feeling of relief. She knew now, in a factual way, that she had been right in her instincts. The tape was proof enough for her, but added to Foley's claim not to have found any drugs in the car, it made her think that she had concrete evidence. Now it was only

71

a question of bypassing the police and the government before justice could be done. She thought of going to the press, but knew the probability of Andy having stitched that one up. No reporters had turned up at Innish, or telephoned. It was unusual for the papers to make no attempt to contact the widow of a prominent figure who died under such dramatic circumstances, even if it was only to take a long-distance photograph of her grieving in the garden.

Armed with a little determination for the first time since Rory's death, she took a pair of secateurs and went into the garden to cut back the wisteria. What she was doing could not be described as pruning, nor had the wisteria any need of pruning, but it helped her to think. By the end of the afternoon the back of her neck was sunburnt and she had decided that her best course of action would be to go to the English tabloids and present the whole thing to them as a scandal. She could play the victimised ex-patriot for all it was worth and leave the rest to their xenophobic hysteria. But not yet. First she wanted a little more evidence, and a few allies.

Sheila and Brendan flew in from Bombay the day before the funeral. They hired a car and turned up at Innish, unannounced, that evening. Helen had never met them before and they matched none of her expectations. Sheila was a very tall, fleshless woman, whose skin was a mass of wrinkles and who had the head movements of a chicken, caused by her having one glass eye, so that she always turned sideways to look at you. Brendan was a short, stocky man, with badly-cut thick hair and a beard. They both wore quite ordinary-looking clothes of loose-fitting khaddar, not the orange robes she had been expecting.

They were both in their late seventies and both without ailment. There was no sign that either of them had ever been beautiful in the way that Rory had been, but if you mixed certain of their unco-ordinated features – Brendan's straight nose and Sheila's height and so on – you could see that Rory had been their son, that he had just been lucky in the way the genes had fused. In another combination of his parents' parts he would have made a whole that was offensive to look at.

Sheila was the sensible one, in that it was Brendan who produced an endless scheme of eccentrically optimistic ideas, while it was Sheila who had to convert them into a practical application or, more usually, rationalise them out of existence. In India and in Germany there were temples with their photographs in the inner sanctuary in place of the usual gods and lingams. But, unlike a lot of the bhagwans and prophets and gurus whose cults have littered the twentieth century, having been elevated to the status of deities within their lifetimes had not inflated their egos unduly. They were still atheists in principle and used their own sanctified condition as evidence that my existence was nothing more than a product of human frailty. Their followers, who were a paradigm of mental frailty, were convinced that the god which was manifest in them was a modest one. I was quietly impressed by all of this, having succumbed to a certain amount of megalomania in my early days, in the days when I still had truck with believers, before I realised that atheists were the only creatures worthy of the trouble.

Within minutes of their arrival Sheila had persuaded Helen to take a bath, despite Brendan's discourse on the inadvisability of washing human hair. He said that he had not washed his own for thirty years, which was why it was so thick and healthy, but he conceded that it was necessary to clean the skin. By the time Helen came downstairs there was food on the table (they had called in at a butcher's on the way) and the windows had been opened to let in the fresh air. She felt a great

73

lightening of spirit because of her cleanness, because of having to hold sociable conversation with strangers, because Brendan and Sheila had been gurus for long enough to know how to make a tortured soul feel at ease.

Having these angels at her table did not, of course, prevent her from talking murder. But she found that with them she could be coherent and plausible. They neither patronised her with false credulity, nor belittled her with scepticism. She played them the tape and told them of Foley's denial of the drugs in the car, and of Andy McGrath's putative silencing of the press. These proofs were easy, because they were tangible. Then she told them what she knew by instinct: that Rory was not a creature of accident.

Then Sheila said, 'My son is dead. I don't know that I have any wish to see the face of his killer.'

Within the span of that statement, Helen had two shocks. The first was that Sheila had called him her son. It was illogical, but while she knew of Sheila as Rory's mother, she had never thought of him as any-one's son. For the first time she thought that someone else might have a genuine share in her grief. The second shock was that Sheila seemed to believe her.

'You believe me?' she said.

Sheila said, 'It isn't a question of my belief. I know that you believe it. That is enough. My son is dead. Knowing who or what killed him will make no difference to that.'

Helen said, 'I've thought about that. I've thought about seeing the face of his killer, but that isn't why I'm doing it. This has nothing to do with vengeance. What I want is my own freedom. My life with Rory has taken away any form of self-respect I ever had, because it was a life with no truth in it, and a life of chasing shadows. I'm not saying it was his fault, although it may be that it was, but I don't think he was bad. He was only ever himself.'

Brendan, who had seemed not to be listening, who had seemed to be counting the plates on the dresser, said, as if he were quoting his own works, 'Concepts of good and evil are a smokescreen. Neither exists, except as a concept. The basis of true morality is passion and indifference.'

Helen said, 'He sounds like Rory, suddenly.'

Sheila said, 'Not now, Brendan. This is neither the time nor the place.'

It was said more as an observation than a rebuke, and caused no discomfort to her husband, who had not left off his study of the dresser. He was not usually so silent, so entrenched in the background, but he felt uncomfortable to be sitting at the table with a fork in his hand and no open-mouthed disciple to swallow his wisdom. He couldn't remember now why they had come. For a funeral, yes, but what was the point of that? Why had they disrupted their lives without question, for the first time in more than twenty years, to watch a box being slid into a hole in the ground? If he had been told that this was the last chance to see Rory alive, he would have made any journey, would have swum rivers to get here. But he couldn't remember what the imperative was that day in Manantavaddi when the telegram came. There had been no discussion, just a universal assumption that they would come here. And now he felt the journey had been a mistake. He felt weakened by it, by airports and airplane seats. He began to feel that he had done a terrible thing by leaving India, that he had forsaken his ideals to participate in a rite of death that had no part in his personal canon. He half-listened to the women talking and wondered how he was going to get through the next few days.

It was that night that Helen's dreams began. They were more realistic than any dreams she had ever had.

They began with her mourning and weeping and then Rory would return to the house, alive but not altogether well, as though he were convalescing. She would feel immense joy and relief at seeing him, and they would talk about banal things, not mentioning where he had been or why he had gone there. Then she would wake, still in a state of euphoria, thinking that his death had been the dream and that he was alive in reality and that everything was going to be all right. It would take her some minutes of consciousness to realise the truth, and then her state of mind would plummet. The dreams were to become regular, but no matter how many times she had them she never got used to the few terrible seconds of the morning when she had to come to terms with his death, again and again, as if for the first time.

On the morning of the funeral she stayed deep in her bed for as long as possible, trying to regain sleep and replay the dream of him being alive. Then Sheila came into her room with a cup of spiced tea, which tasted like Christmas pudding, but was not unpleasant at that time of the morning. There were sounds of activity from downstairs. Kay had arrived with a carload of food to feed the mourners. Brendan was polishing glasses and setting them in rows in the dining room.

Helen said, 'I dreamt he was alive.'

Sheila said, 'I dreamt he was two years old again. He was lost and I went out to look for him. And then I saw his fat little legs sticking out of a ditch. He wasn't dead, only stuck. I was still pulling on his legs when I woke up.'

'Did Brendan dream of him?'

Sheila answered, cryptically, 'Brendan's mind is his own. And it isn't what it was.'

Scores of people turned up for the funeral, and then hundreds, until the field was black with mourners and the lanes locked with their cars. He was buried under the boughs of an oak tree where the land sloped down to the estuary, and the whole thing seemed a little too picturesque to be real. The service was taken by a man who called himself Father Cooper. He wasn't the parish priest, and no one was quite sure where he had come from, except that he had turned up on the Wednesday morning claiming to be an old friend of Rory's. He had a good strong voice, capable of wrenching tears from anyone not already affected by the atmosphere. Government ministers and senior policemen and the stars of international architecture draped their arms on the lower boughs of the tree and kept their faces turned from their chauffeurs. Corinna, looking out of place in her black post-Goth trappings, had her arm held by David as if he thought she was in danger of running away. He held Sid in the crook of his other arm. Corinna looked more terrified than sad, and David kept a constant whisper in her ear, 'It's all right now. It's all right. It won't be long now and we can go home. It's all right. He can't hurt you.' David had had misgivings about coming to the funeral at all, but she had said she wanted to, and he would see to it that she got through it. Kay was there, but not Jody. He had put on black clothes in the morning but would come no further than the front door. Moby Donlan stood at the back with the curious and Alan Kehoe came near the centre with the interested. He watched Corinna and he watched the coffin and his right leg shook as if with the cold, even though he was sweating in the heat.

Rory Dixon's mother, his wife and his mistress stood, three in a row, at the foot of the grave. Naturally each of them was weeping, but Helen was being held up by the other two. And then as the coffin was being lowered Helen let a great scream out of her, like the scream of a woman in labour, and had to be restrained from following her husband into the hole. The atmosphere was broken after that, changing from sadness to

77

spectacle. But it gave Foley the diversion he needed to slip away, and no one saw the fat sergeant disappear over the hill, from where he could get back into the house unseen.

Once there, he had two objectives. The first was easy enough. The tape was still in the machine and the machine was in Rory's workroom, where he had seen it. The second objective was trickier, since it involved getting up the narrow steps into the attic. But the stuff was where it should have been, below a floorboard at the back of the water tank. He just had time to get it out of the house and safely stowed in the squad car before the first of the funeral party began to arrive at the door.

Alan Kehoe had been identified as the boy who had found the body, and pointed out to Sheila, who asked him up to the house. She also insisted, it being the first time she had seen her grandchild and her great-grandchild, that Corinna and David and Sid come back, and made certain of it by carrying Sid into the house herself. In all there were seventy or eighty people who came in for a drink, chattering about the heat of the day and the likelihood of thunderstorms. Since Helen's theatrics at the graveside there was an air of mild titillation and expectation among them. They watched her to see what she might do next, but she seemed to have regained her composure, and was wandering from room to room with a sherry bottle in one hand and a whisky bottle in the other, filling glasses and smiling with an appropriate weakness at condolences. As she moved, she caused a buffer zone of silence to travel with her which, happily, she chose to treat as a mark of respect. The truth, she knew, was that they were all afraid of her. Not only was she marked with death, but in their eyes she was mad to boot. From time to time she caught Sheila's eye, or the two of them spoke together for a moment, and it was from Sheila that she drew her strength. Sheila was the only other one who knew what sort of man Rory had been in reality, and only Sheila could be her friend. Brendan was in a corner, explaining to a couple of farmers the value of human excrement as a fertilizer.

Alan Kehoe wanted to speak to Corinna, but was afraid to go near her while her husband was by her side and the child was being admired. There was no one else he knew in the house. Awkward as he felt when standing on his own in the middle of the room, he felt worse whenever someone took pity on him and tried to speak to him. On these occasions he blushed to near-purple and could only answer in monosyllables. He always tried to stand in Corinna's line of sight, hoping that she would come over and speak to him, but she never even looked at him.

After twenty minutes or so, David asked Corinna if they might leave and she said that she wanted to stay, but that he should go home with the baby. He would have liked to stand up to her, would have liked to ask her why she wanted to be without him in the house she hated, but he didn't have any words to question her with. And he was afraid, knowing her, that she might tell him the truth. He looked about him at the other men in the room. There were men of all shapes and ages and all of them, presumably, were capable of going upstairs with her. He was afraid to know and he was afraid of his ignorance. He caught Alan Kehoe's eye and Alan looked away in embarrassment. But David interpreted that not as a sign of guilt, but as the mark of a man who felt as displaced as himself among vol-au-vents and dainty speakers. He crossed the nervous fisherboy off the list of his wife's potential lovers. And then he took Sid from the arms of the child's latest admirer and made his way to the door.

He passed close by Helen, who said, 'You're going?' All he could answer was 'Thanks,' and made to go on, towards the glare of the sun in the front doorway.

'Wait,' she said. 'How would you feel about living in Dublin?'

It was such an odd question, at such an odd time, that he didn't even think of formulating an answer.

'I'm going to stay here,' she said. 'You and Corinna can have the house in Dublin if you want it.'

'We have a house,' he said.

'Think about it, anyway. Talk to Corinna.'

'You could talk to her yourself.'

That was a vicious thing to say, and he was aware of it. He walked away from her and into the sun, towards where he had parked his brother's car.

Not long after he had gone, Corinna went upstairs and Alan followed her, catching up with her on the first landing.

'You don't remember me,' he said.

'You're the great swimmer,' she said, looking at him in that flat, discomfiting way she had, making him feel as though his flies were open.

'I didn't know you were married. The other night.' He knew by the way she was looking at him that he should never have started this conversation, but now the journey back was further than the journey ahead.

'So?' she said. 'I knew I was married. And you know now.'

He was blocked by her. There was nothing he could say, but at the same time he was on his own with her and that might be a thing that would never happen again. He stood his ground and tried to look her in the eye. The fear in him was transforming itself to anger.

'So,' she said, 'what's this all supposed to be about? Do you want me to fuck you again?'

'For Jesus' sake. It's supposed to be your father's funeral.'

'It's what he would have done.'

'I just wanted to talk.'

'So?' she said. 'Talk.'

'I can't,' he said.

'Go away then. I have something to do. And don't worry about it. No one can talk. They only think they can. There's no such thing as talk.'

She looked so sad and so angry as she spoke that he thought for one second that he had got through to her. And then he looked at her again and saw how irredeemable she was, and he wanted nothing more than to fuck her again at that moment, and he realised that that was what he had wanted all along, and he regretted not having said yes when she asked him. It was too late now.

'Yes,' he said.

'Yes what?'

'Yes to what you asked me a minute ago.'

'Stop coddin' yourself,' she said. 'That isn't what you want at all.' And she walked away from him down the landing and into the first bathroom on her left, the bathroom she had used in her childhood, with the big white bath she had been sitting in years ago when she had started her first menstruation.

After she had left Alan standing at the top of the stairs and locked herself into the bathroom, Corinna lay in the bath, fully clothed, knowing that courage was deserting her. She had come with everything she needed. She took a razor blade out of one pocket, and lay it in the soap dish and looked at it for a long time. She tried to persuade herself how good it would be if she did it exactly as she had planned. To fill the bath with warm water and lie in it, without undressing or even taking her shoes off. There was nothing to be proved by her being found naked. To take the blade in her left hand and, keeping her right arm below the level of the water, cut deep into the wrist and lie back and watch.

81

It would be painless. No sensation of losing blood, just the spectacle of her blood billowing through the water like milk in tea, and a growing feeling of weakness that would not be unpleasant. No movement, no turning back. If she moved she might cause herself pain. She had been causing herself pain for so many years and this was supposed to be an escape from it. If she died in peace she might rest in peace, thinking about heaven in the last moments, and then thinking about nothing, going from one coherent thought to no thought at all. The blood still flowing and the water darkening and she halfway between unconsciousness and death.

The more she thought about it the less courage she had to do it. Several times she reached for the taps to turn them on, and drew back. She took a piece of paper from her jacket and read it, and wished she hadn't written it. What on earth was the point of a suicide note when the whole point of wanting to do this was that there was nothing, no one left in this life? She had thought of that before. She had addressed the note to her father, but now that seemed like a puerile act of attention-seeking. Who did she want to explain herself to? Not to Sid, certainly. He would be better off believing whatever story they chose to fabricate for him when he came to the age of asking questions. And even if children were better off knowing the truth, she didn't think that she was a fit person to impart it. She wondered if she should flush the note down the lavatory, if getting rid of the note would leave her free to use the razor blade.

There was an almost inaudible tapping on the door. She stood up out of the bath and left the note on a roll of lavatory paper, as silently as she could, hoping that whoever it was would go away. If only she had done it, she could be dead by now, and not have to wonder who was tapping, and not have to see them, and not have to speak to them. And then she thought that perhaps it was as well, since whoever was tapping might have raised an alarm and she might have been discovered and rescued, and an attempted suicide would be added to the reasons for which old women looked at her in the street as if she had two heads.

There was another tapping. It was being done with the discretion, not of someone who wanted to use the bathroom, but of someone who knew she was in there. She thought it must be the fishing boy, come for his pound of flesh.

'Who is it?' she said.

And a voice said in a whisper, 'It's me.'

And thinking that she could forget about dying that day, she turned the key in the lock and said, 'It's open. What do you want?'

Bloodbath

I know that I'm supposed to love all my children equally, but who does? Of course you can love them equally in the abstract sense (and over the years I have become very abstract indeed), but it becomes inevitable that one child will be better company than another, or more beautiful, or simply capable of making you laugh. When you get to my age, and you won't, you become a little selfish about your pleasures. I got rather tired of the human race, and Rory Dixon was a breath of fresh air. He was the creature he was intended to be. He was an intelligent animal. Wholly intelligent and wholly animal. His primary motive in everything was passion, and he applied his passion with a deviance, with an originality that was beautiful to watch. That he was the cause of evil is indisputable, since evil is endemic in the world and any cause at all will have some evil effect. But he was not an evil creature, nor could the spurious ideal of good have been applied to him. He was curious and he had the courage of his curiosity. Given that courage, curiosity is the greatest of human virtues. The sin of Adam was not one of curiosity, but of his subsequent cowardice (and the way he blamed the girlie). If, having gained his knowledge, he had stood naked before his maker, who knows? Not that the Adam and Eve story is any more than a metaphor: a metaphor I approve of, without approving of the ways in which it has been applied.

Adams and Eves and metaphors are ten-a-penny, but there were never many like Rory. I was sorry to lose him, and there is nothing I can do about getting him back. But I still have some interest in those he left behind. In some ways his life won't be over until the lives of those he has touched and affected are finished. The works of Rory Dixon are not only in steel-clad buildings across the world, but in the souls of those other beings who were seduced by him.

Let's not confine our definition of seduction to the sexual. The sexual is, admittedly, the most rewarding and, to a watcher of men, the most interesting form of seduction, since sex is the universal metaphor of all existence and all existence is, in turn, dependent on sex (we will come to apomixis later). A priori and a posteriori; chicken and egg, some might say, though without having given the matter much thought. It should be obvious to any fool in a post-Darwinian society that eggs evolved long before chickens. You might use the same argument to say that sexuality and the genetic imperative evolved long before the appearance of man. But who is to say that other creatures do not, and have not always, used their sexuality as a metaphor? Who can say that a stegasaurus had no need of metaphors, of his equivalent of painting, music and pornography? It is widely held that the animal and the spiritual are opposite. For animal you may often read sexual. That cannot be so. There was never a human who was pure of mind who achieved anything in this world. The effort involved in purity of mind will destroy the spirit. Thomas Aquinas was a filthy old louse in spite of all that repression. If we are to set states of consciousness in opposition to each other we can more easily put the spiritual and the animal into alliance, and place a dry, barren, incurious state of perfection across an unbridgeable chasm. Remember, after all, it was in another well-known metaphor that the Virgin Mary got fucked by the Holy Spirit (I told you we'd deal with apomixis).

But we are talking about seduction, and we are talking about Rory Dixon, always about Rory Dixon, and we are looking for his thumbprints in the flesh of others, and we have left the unfortunate Corinna high and dry in the last moments of her life, as her murderer turns the handle of the bathroom door. Given that, we may as well be hung for a sheep as a lamb and leave that animation suspended a while longer, and while she is alive take a glance at that distorted mind and how Rory Dixon catalysed it, first to catharsis and finally to cathexis.

He was, let us choose the word carefully, her lover. Throughout her childhood they had as good, as normal a relationship as can prevail between a father and a daughter. As far as she was aware, he never lied to her and she trusted him. He noticed, of course he noticed, when her breasts began to swell, but like any good father he transposed a protective indignation for any inkling of his own desire. He had none of the acceptable clichéd reasons to become a child abuser; he was no control freak with a complex about the size of his penis. Fatherhood was the only area in life where he was happy to be normal in the knowledge, gained from his own childhood, that normality is what children crave above everything. The first time it was an accident, and the second time it was less of an accident. The first time was in the week before her seventeenth birthday and the second time was in the week after it.

They were alone in the house in Dublin, and Rory had taken a couple of purple hearts, back in the days when E was still wonderful, and they were watching television (MTV I think) and Rory opened a bottle of wine; very good wine – a Grand Cru 1985 Pomerol. Corinna, knowing that her father was on something or other and would be an easy touch, said that now she was nearly seventeen she should be allowed to drink, and he said of course, this wine is so wonderful, and she got a glass, and because he was on E and every sip seemed to take an hour, Corinna drank most of the bottle and, being unused to wine, became very drunk indeed. She fell asleep, snuggled against her father on the sofa, and he began to think that that wouldn't do and he carried her up to bed, and took off her shoes – in those days she still wore shoes – and undressed her to her underwear and put her between the sheets, like any father should do for any daughter, and he kissed her goodnight and she smelled so incredible and her skin felt so incredible but he should have known it was only the E that made him think that, but he switched out her bedside light, thinking that he felt so good he would stay beside her a few minutes, and thinking how lucky he was that he loved his daughter so much, and how incredible it was that you could love someone so much without sex coming into it, and as he thought that, she moved, and he became aware that he had a coiled erection straining the seams in his trousers, and he did think that he should leave then, but he wanted to be near her for one more minute, and she moved again, and somehow they kissed, and somehow they became naked, and somehow he put his head between her thighs, and somehow she kissed the head of his penis, and somehow it seemed as if she was doing everything in her sleep, because she never opened her eyes and her breathing was deep, hot on his balls, and all he could think was how much he loved her.

He had a vague memory of gathering his clothes and going to his own room, but the E had taken him to a state where he was incapable of thought, of deduction, of forecast. It was only instinct that told him he mustn't wake up naked in his daughter's bed, his morning horn pressed against her backside. He slept, and he woke euphoric, or as euphoric as you can be with a blinding headache. He tried to think what he had done to make himself so euphoric and then he remembered that he had fucked Corinna, and that she had fucked him, and that was the beginning of the most terrible day of his life. There are people who regret things all the time, but he had never regretted anything until now; until now he had been happy with the responsibility of all his actions. Whether it is that the first time has to be the worst time, or whether it was because he had done such a terrible thing, had allowed such a terrible thing to happen, regret hit him like a wall of concrete falling on his face, and he almost panicked. He got dressed and went to look for her, but she wasn't in the house. He questioned the girl who came in to do the washing up, and tried to sound casual, but he thought that the wrong he had done must surely be visible on his face. The girl said that Corinna had left for Innish on the morning bus.

And Rory said, 'Was she all right?'

And the girl said, 'Yeah, she was grand.'

The whole of that day he was paralysed. He desperately wanted to see Corinna, to see if she was all right, to know how bad the damage was. Until then he could have no idea what to do, or whether there was anything that could be done. But it was evident that she had left for Innish to get away from him. He wondered if she would tell Helen about it. It was possible, but unlikely. Corinna had never been close to her mother, not close in that way. If she were ever in trouble it would be him she would turn to, normally. He should follow her, or he should phone, but he couldn't deal with the idea of Helen being part of whatever might ensue. He spent that day in fear and, being unused to fear, it was fairly terrible for him.

Corinna returned the following evening, and everything seemed normal, in their greetings, in their conversation. That much was a relief: she seemed unchanged, outwardly. But still he had to know. He couldn't pretend forever that it had never happened. He began to apologise, to make reference to the happenings of the other night, but she looked at him blankly and slightly warily, and he began to realise that she had no memory of it at all; or that she had blanked it from her mind; or that her only way of coping with it was to pretend to have no memory of it. He left it at that, thinking that it was lucky; it was the best possible result. There was remission, there was a second chance, and if he was careful in the future, everything was going to be fine.

But then days later it happened again, not exactly the same way, but in similar circumstances, and it began to happen regularly, once a month or so, always with her living the pretence that she had no memory of it happening at all, even though sometimes they were both stone cold sober. And it was a thing of pleasure while it was happening, and the rest of life became hell for both of them. That was when Corinna began to get into trouble: shoplifting and hanging out in Denny Power's and wearing Goth clothes and stealing her father's stash of dope to smoke with her new friends. She failed her Leaving Certificate, failing even to turn up for any of the exams, and said that she hated Dublin and began to live at Innish all the time, even in the winter when she would be alone in the house, apart from whatever motorcycling drip she brought back for the night. If she was trying to break her relationship with her father, it worked. She changed so much that there could hardly be a conversation between them, let alone an orgasm, and he felt helpless watching the change because he knew that he had been the cause. And then even Innish became unbearable to Corinna, and she met David Kennedy and fell pregnant and moved into the back bedroom of his parents' house.

Always, even as a snooty upper-middle-class Dublin teenager, she had been the sort of girl who gained her greatest pleasure from reading the morbid parts of Keats and Dickinson and mooning about in Glasnevin cemetery, alighting on monuments to compose her own odes to suicide and death. As a fixation it was no more bizarre or worrying than the preoccupations of other girls with horses or groupieism, and no doubt she would have grown out of it in the course of a normal sexual development. But development of any kind was blocked by the unspeakable nature of her love for her father, and it began to seem natural to her that everything that had happened had brought her closer to a state of mind where suicide was a realistic possibility, and not the dramatisation of a romantic girl. In my opinion she would never, in fact, have done it. She was possessed of the desperation but not the power, and her desperation was that of the lost and not the driven. She was young enough to mend and had she survived she might have mended in time, under the steadiness of David Kennedy's tolerance of her. Her ceremony in the bathroom was no more than that, even though she believed that through Rory's death she was finally independent enough to do her duty by herself, and that duty was her own obliteration, and the funeral was an auspicious moment for the act. So we are back where we left her, watching the door handle turn.

Downstairs, the levity which follows hard on the heels of a burying was making itself heard in groups and corners. The funeral crowd was thinning and those who remained were becoming more cheerful by the minute, as outrageous stories were told about Rory's life and adventures, as drink was knocked back and heads were thrown back in laughter. Helen at last had found the antidote to commiseration, and whenever her hand was pressed and she heard the words 'I'm sorry for your trouble,' in that low, confidential voice which is reserved for those words alone, she would not answer 'I know that,' as custom demanded, but say 'Really?' in a voice which left her interlocutor to withdraw in silent embarrassment.

'Such ignorance,' they said to one another. 'She never had manners.'

How could she have manners, in a society where the rules were unwritten, and where the worse manners of all were to be seen to acquire manners you weren't born with? Helen had been born into the strait-jacket of English suburbia, into a house of doilies and pardon, from which she had been liberated by the classlessness of the King's Road in the sixties. Her social skills hovered somewhere between the pertness of her up-bringing and the looseness of an art school, with the gloss of an impeccable taste in material things thrown over it. She had assumed, like a lot of foreigners, that the easy-going surface of Irish society was indicative of social anarchy, and once she became aware of the rigidity of Ireland's social skeleton it was too late to change her behaviour, and she was too embittered to want to change it.

The other misfit in the gathering, Alan Kehoe, would have left the house as soon as he had come downstairs, but he was cornered by Brendan, who had a lot to tell him about the sex lives of fish and the parallels to be drawn between their amorousness and world politics.

Dan Fieselbaum, Rory's junior partner, and Kieran Dunne, his solicitor, were in deep, humourless conversation. They had bad news to break to Helen and they were plotting the best way to go about it. The architectural practice was swimming in debt, both houses were mortgaged to the hilt, and Rory's personal overdraft was standing at four hundred thousand, more or less. Were Rory living, these problems would not be insuperable. He had been in worse fixes before. There were contracts in the pipeline which, if they came through, would sort things out, but it was doubtful whether the clients would go ahead with the commissions without Rory's presiding genius. He had died intestate, and so the bulk of the responsibility fell to Helen, who had shown no signs of financial acumen so far. The two men had just begun to move in Helen's direction to begin the process of letting her know that she was not a rich widow, when the commotion began.

Father Cooper should have been the first to notice, since it was while his head was reared back and his mouth open in a guffaw that the first drop fell onto his quivering tongue. But then, maybe men of his profession are used to the taste of sacrificial blood. A moment later, Kay thought she saw something falling in her glass, but was so unsure about it that she tasted the wine to see if there was any difference. Then she looked up to the ceiling.

A drop of pink liquid lets go its hold of the plaster and landed across the bridge of her nose. She squealed, more in surprise than alarm. The ceiling was dotted with these pink drops, quivering against gravity. At the sound of her voice, everyone in the room looked upwards and a good many of them were rewarded with drips of watered-down blood on their foreheads and their chins. There were a few seconds of silent uncertainty, and then it was Alan who suggested that this might be more than the plumbing gone wrong. He knew the colour of watery blood from seeing it wash across the deck of the boat, day after day.

'It's blood,' was all he said, in a quiet voice, feeling that he had no authority to make this suggestion, and having no idea what should be done once he had made it. People looked from one to another, waiting for the next step to be decided, sidestepping the drips while Kay wiped the liquid from her eyes with the back of her hand. It was Sheila who first made for the door, having counted who was in the room and knowing whose blood it must be. And all the others, as if she had given them a signal, moved at once in a tight pack of black-clad bodies, swarming after her up the stairs.

Corinna was long dead when the funeral party came hammering on the bathroom door; when Alan Kehoe, blind with fear, kicked at the lock until it broke under the heel of his shoe. In an instant the room was full of policemen, politicians, architects and doctors (including, oddly enough, Dublin's most eminent haematologist), but nothing could be done for her. It was hard for anyone to speak, and the most noticeable sound was that of feet squelching in the sodden carpet. It was Sheila who thought to turn the taps off, and Sheila who saw that sheet of paper on the lavatory roll, folded and addressed to Rory.

Corinna was submerged to her chin in the water, and her throat was cut. The water in the bath had cleared to pale kir pink. Her clothes had been pulled about, but not badly. There was a general assumption, an unspoken consensus that she had killed herself, because of the locked door and because of her Goth, attention-seeking appearance. It put her beyond what those with more conventional lives were prepared to comprehend as an appetite for any kind of a life at all, and so, to them, she had been a potential suicide from the moment she first painted her fingernails black and put a stud in her nose. To the crowd in the bathroom it would have been astonishing if anyone had taken the trouble to murder her, but suicide was perceived as a natural end to the life she had caused herself and a culmination of the grief she had caused others. There were few who could see that her troubles had stemmed from her inability to cause the quorum of griefs which validate an existence. There were few who would admit that it is only by the grief of others that we know we are loved. So Corinna's life, in the eyes of most of those who saw her dead, was a failure of her own choosing, and the note that Sheila picked up was not so much a confirmation as an inevitable element in the event.

'I'll take that,' Foley said. 'It's evidence.'

Sheila glared at him. She said, 'It's my grand-daughter. It is addressed to my son.'

There was no means, given the emotional force with which she had spoken and the presence of so many people, by which he could argue with her.

The note was ambiguous in some ways. It read:

'There is no excuse for what you did to me and no excuse for what I did to you. Murder is murder and love is nothing so definite. There are excuses for love and excuses is all they are. It wasn't a secret because of shame, but because no one would have seen what it was. They would have called it abuse, without seeing that, weak as I was, you were weaker. Someone would have killed you sooner or later, but I always thought I would have killed myself sooner. I'm writing this in case I don't see you over there. If there is justice the two of us will be put in the same hell. But this is in case over there doesn't exist. It isn't for you. It's for me, for once.'

Sheila read it, and passed it to Helen, who was leaning against the sink, her face as pale as that of her blood-drained daughter. Helen read it and said two words.

'The bitch,' she said.

Granny Takes a Trip

It didn't make the front page of the English tabloids, since it coincided with the latest royal adultery, but it got more attention than the man who had been sexually abusing his Bedlington terrier in Doncaster, and the Commodore Hotel did a roaring trade as tabloid journalists and photographers settled in to follow the developments.

The story, as it was leaked to the media and reported, was first that Corinna, having suffered abuse at the hands of her father, had murdered him and then taken her own life in remorse and in the presence of half the Irish government. That much was Helen's doing, and that was the way she would have chosen to interpret the events of the night before. It was an interpretation that would also have been the choice of a few other interested parties, as far as damage limitation was concerned. If it had to be admitted, finally, that Rory had been murdered, then it was better than his killer was dead and unable to stand trial. Still, eventually, there would have to be inquests. Sergeant Foley was not in the best of positions. Detectives were sent from Dublin and he lost all control of the situation. His best hope was that the mismanagement of the case so far would be put down to the incompetence of the rural police, and he played the gormless innocent with all the skills of a veteran Machiavellian underling. Luckily for him, he had taken and destroyed the tape from the answering machine, so it could not be brought as evidence that he had tried to suppress an investigation. It was unfortunate that four other people had heard it, but the voice had been so distorted that none of them could agree exactly what had been said. It could, they all admitted, have been Corinna's voice, since she had spoken with a rich, almost masculine timbre.

It was Sheila who first began to suspect that the detectives, despite their seeming thoroughness, were inclined to gloss over certain loose ends. To begin with, she was as bewildered as anyone by the turn of events. She went to bed that night and slept the deep sleep of shock and exhaustion, oblivious that Brendan was lying by her side with his eyes wide open, muttering in Malayalam. She woke early and with a start, the way she always did. She reached for her husband's testicles to begin the process of making love, as they had done every morning for more than fifty years. It had become almost a form of meditation. The rhythm of those seven minutes of coitus gave her a chance to think what she would have to do during the day; the pleasure of waking with a fuck as pleasant and necessary to her as waking to a cup of coffee is to some.

She could feel a difference in Brendan. His body was the same and his movements were the same. He had always been a languorous lover, and so old age had done nothing to cramp his style; he had never had a wonderful body, and so a few wrinkles here and there were nothing to complain about. But this morning there was something absurd about him, something wrong with his expression. He kissed her like a schoolboy who was up to no good, and not like a veteran of the sexual revolution. She held his face in her two hands, her thumbs pushing the deep skin into folds up to his eyes, and looked at him.

'Are you all right?' she said.

'There is no,' he said.

'No what? There is no what?'

'Nothing,' he said. 'There is nothing.'

He put his head against her bony chest and she thought he might cry, waited for the sensation of his tears coming across her breast.

'We should never have come,' he said.

'No,' she said.

She took one of his hands and counted the liver spots on the back of it, and watched how the skin was shiny in places like the skin of a half-scaled fish, and how thick his fingernails had become over the years, and she felt that he must be old. Not that she had ever been blind to his ageing, but she had always seen him as himself first and his age second. She realised now that there must come a time when age overrides the person, when old people stop being themselves and become the same as each other. The back of his hand was not very different from the back of her own. For some time now he had been going soft. Soft was the word she thought of. The man she had known as her husband was slipping away, and she was left with this old person, interchangeable in all probability with half the old men in the country. He still had thick hair, and a cock that did its duty by her in the mornings, but how long would that last? How long before his prostate went and he had to have the old man's operation? And what then? Companionship? She could get companionship from an animal. What she wanted was intimacy, and the intimacy she wanted was the one she got from his unclothed body in her bed, and his unageing member between the walls of her vagina. And where did love come into that? She loved him fine, as much as you can love anyone, but it was him she loved, not the old carcass with the soft brain that was being left in his place.

She may have thought that she was thinking all these

things, but in the extraordinary way that it will sometimes happen, the outcome of her thoughts was not even related to the subject. It may have been that her subconscious was working in parallel with her conscious mind, or it may have been that she had come to some resolution in her dreams, and suddenly remembered it at that moment. Whatever it was, the thing that she said having counted the liver-spots on her husband's hands was, 'She couldn't have killed herself. What's making us all so stupid? Nobody kills themself by cutting their throat. And what about the key? The door was locked, but I saw no key. I remember looking at the door, thinking how easy it had been for that boy to kick it open, and wondering whether it was a bad lock or a strong leg. There was no key on the inside. Did you see a key?'

She thought she heard him mumble 'No', or something like it. His head was still pressed into her chest. But she hadn't been asking him for the sake of an answer. She pushed him away from her and went to the bathroom. Luckily there was more than one and she didn't have to perform her ablutions while standing on the carpet that was soaked with her grandchild's blood.

She found Helen in the drawing room surrounded by newspapers, reviewing the results of her work like any good publicist. Sheila glanced at a few of the headlines.

'That was quick,' she said. 'I wonder how they found out so soon.'

Helen didn't exactly smile. There was too much tragedy in the air for smiling, but she did manage to look a small bit pleased with herself, as though she had managed to achieve something in spite of a general opinion that she was incapable of achievement. She said, 'I told them. I thought it was time the truth got an airing.'

Picking up one of the papers, Sheila said, 'That's a dangerous presumption.' There was a facsimile of the suicide note printed on the page. Helen must have been faxing and phoning the whole of the previous evening, while the rest of them were slumped in shock.

'What do you mean?'

'The thing that overturns a fiction won't necessarily be the truth. The truth, if it exists at all, is not a robust animal. Lies are more easily replaced with more lies.'

'I thought you were on my side.'

'I probably am. But we can't be certain until you find out which side you're on yourself.'

'Sweet Jesus,' Helen said. 'This isn't a bloody ashram. I've had it up to here with half-fucking-baked philosophising.'

Sheila closed the paper and folded it. 'Wait and see,' she said. 'Even the police can't be stupid enough to go on thinking that Corinna's death was suicide.'

'But you were there. Everyone saw it.'

'How was the door locked? There was no key in the bathroom. I know. I've just checked again to be sure.'

'Maybe she threw it out the window?'

'Why would she? In any case, she didn't. I've had a look outside.'

'Why would anyone kill her?'

'Why would anyone kill Rory?'

'She killed Rory.'

So far, Helen had been on Sheila's blind side. Now Sheila turned and looked at her with her good eye. 'That remains to be seen,' she said.

Helen was fighting to keep a grip on herself. She wanted Corinna to have been the one who murdered Rory. She needed an excuse to hate the daughter she had never liked anyway, an excuse not to have to mourn her. And as for the other things that were implied in the note – the implication that Rory's relationship with his daughter had been abusive, the understanding

101

between the two of them from which Helen had been excluded – they were a vindication of the suspicions she had always had that Rory led a secret life.

'What do we do?' She heard the desperation in her voice as she almost begged that question of Sheila.

'Nothing. Not just now. The detectives said they would be back at ten, and if they haven't worked it out for themselves by then, we tell them what we think.'

'What you think.'

'Sorry. What I think.'

The men from Dublin were not, in any obvious way, more intelligent or competent than Foley and the rural Gardai, but they were outsiders and there was a possibility that they would be looking for evidence instead of covering the trail of their own misdoings. They arrived at Innish after a busy morning. The blue Spider had been retrieved from the wrecker's yard and properly examined. It was found that the brakes had been tampered with, not once, but twice. The first cut in the cable had been repaired, and then the cable had been cut again. That was a source of great puzzlement. If there had been an earlier attempt to murder Rory, would the killer have used exactly the same method the second time? And had Rory been aware of the first attempt? If it had been Corinna, had she, in her unstable state of mind, regretted the first attempt and repaired it herself, and then regretted again and made a second cut? But the repair seemed to have been done professionally, and there was no evidence that Corinna had any mechanical training. Also, it would seem that all Corinna's movements were accounted for in the twenty-four hours that preceded Rory's death. There was little likelihood that she was the killer.

As Sheila had predicted, the detectives were sceptical about the suicide. The scene of death was an investigator's nightmare, because of the number of people who had crowded into the bathroom. The only evidence for suicide was her temperament and the note, which was covered with the fingerprints of at least half-a-dozen people and had been put through the fax machine twenty times by Helen before it fell into the hands of Authority. Foley, who had allowed all this to happen, had also allowed most of the witnesses to disperse back to their homes all over the country without questioning them. It was unfortunate that the two senior gardai who had been present at the funeral had returned to Dublin before the discovery of Corinna's body, since a little professionalism at that moment might have made for a case that was manageable if not comprehensible.

It was amazing what a thorough search of that house revealed. Years of hedonism had left forgotten acid tabs in little boxes and twists of cocaine fallen down the back of drawers and scraps of dope that had been put away for safekeeping by people who were too stoned to remember where they had hidden them. There was a pile of good old seventies porn videos covered in dust at the bottom of a wardrobe and used-up tubes of K-Y in a locked drawer in the spare room. Poppers, syringes, handcuffs and all the other detritus of once-fashionable experiments were taken out of their hidey-holes and sealed into clear plastic bags. Beneath one loose floorboard there was seven thousand pounds in old notes, wrapped in a sock; money that had been hidden for an emergency in a time of plenty and forgotten by the time the emergency came. It was a satisfying haul – evidence of a life that had not been taken for granted. I doubt if they would find as much if they got a warrant to ransack heaven.

Helen, when questioned, of course denied all knowledge of these things. They must have been Rory's, she said, and how could she have possibly known of their existence when housework had never been part of her function in life?

103

'What is your function in life?' the detective said.

Helen felt under no obligation to dignify that question with an answer, even if she had been capable of thinking of one.

For the fourth time the detective asked her, 'Do you have any idea who might have killed your husband?'

'I've told you,' she said. 'Corinna did it. She admitted it in that note.'

'And if it wasn't her? Who then?'

'Of course it was her. Perhaps she didn't actually cut the brakes herself. David could have done that. Have you spoken to David? She controlled him. He would have done anything for her. And he hated us. Corinna turned him against us.'

'Mr Kennedy is helping us at the barracks in Gavinston.'

'Has he told you that he trained as a car mechanic, before he went into the post office?'

The detective made no reply to that, but wrote something down on his notepad. He said, 'And who might have killed your daughter?'

'She killed herself. I told you what I think.'

'She may have killed herself.' The detective was being patient with her. 'But if we supposed that she didn't. What then?'

'David, I suppose. She had driven him to murder and he was afraid of her and wanted to be free of her.'

'David had left the house before she went upstairs. You've confirmed that yourself. He went home with the child.'

'He could have come back.'

'What would he have done with the child?'

'You're the detective.'

The detective changed tack. 'Mrs Dixon, would you say you had a happy marriage?'

'Oh, come on,' she said. 'I'm not falling for that. Couldn't you even phrase it with a little more originality?

You've been watching too much television. It isn't any of your business, but we had a good marriage, and I didn't kill him.'

'What about all this?' The detective nodded towards the pile of plastic bags on the table between them, and focused on the squeezed-out tubes of lubricant.

'What about it? I told you. I knew nothing about any of this. If I had known we might have been unhappy. But I didn't. As far as I was concerned our marriage was sheer bloody bliss.'

'I've heard otherwise, Mrs Dixon.'

'From whom? Who could know except me, and him? Nobody knows what really goes on, do they?'

'That is more or less what I was thinking, Mrs Dixon.'

It is, I know, part of the function of an interrogator to be blameless, holier-than-thou, certainly holier than his subject, but I did admire the acting skills of this particular detective, a man who paid weekly visits to a transvestite hooker in Leeson Street, whom he paid for the privilege of rimming her, a man who had beaten his wife senseless on several occasions and who had disowned his eldest son for marrying a Jewess. Never mind what Rabbie Burns said. Wouldn't it be altogether extraordinary if others could see us as we are ourselves? What Mr Burns didn't know was that neither gift is within the scope of my giving. You'll just have to sort it out for yourselves.

Helen was not altogether concerned with whether this man had any justification for the high moral tone he was taking with her. She herself was acting a part now in self-defence. She knew that a spouse is a prime suspect. She knew that if Corinna had an alibi and David had an alibi she would be the next most obvious choice. She knew that if her marriage was aired in a courtroom people would wonder why there hadn't been a killing in the household years ago. She knew what was coming next.

'If you don't mind me asking, Mrs Dixon, where were you the day your husband died?'

'I was here. Where else would I be?'

'All day? Was anyone here with you?'

She could sense danger. The detective was speaking more nonchalantly than was natural. The other detective was sitting completely still somewhere behind her, as if he were hoping that she would forget he was there, as if they were hoping that she might let something slip if she thought there was no witness to it.

'I don't like what you are implying,' she said.

'I'm not implying anything. There are facts to be established.'

'In that case.' She turned around to look at the other detective, to let him know that she hadn't forgotten his presence, nor that she was outnumbered. 'In that case, I would like the facts to be established in the presence of my solicitor.'

'Fine.' It was said in a tone that was friendly enough, if slightly exasperated, but at the same time he managed to look at her as if she were already the accused, as if a demand for legal representation were proof of guilt.

They interviewed Brendan, but all they got from him was a discourse on the worship of the water-buffalo by the tribals near Manantavaddi. His memory of the funeral was hazy. He couldn't recall the names of anyone who was there, let alone who had been in the room at any particular time.

Sheila was more helpful.

'I've been thinking,' she said. 'I know you have questions, but I am an old woman and if you don't let me say what I think first, then it may have gone out of my head by the time you've finished with me. I take it that you have worked out that Corinna could not have committed suicide? Good. The first thing that we need to do is work out the time it happened. No, don't interrupt. I know people like you are irritated by amateurs, and I am not assuming that you haven't thought of any of this yourselves. But I have a suggestion. I would have thought that whoever killed my grandchild did it while she was already in the bath, but before the bath was full of water.'

'Why?'

'Because the water was not a necessary factor in the act of killing. It was added later to make the suicide business more plausible. That is why the taps were left running, to reinforce the idea that she was distracted enough to have done it herself. So, assuming all that, we should run a test to see how long it takes the bath to overflow and seep through the ceiling. I can remember how far the tap was turned on when we came into the bathroom. And if we can get an approximate time I could probably tell you who might have been upstairs when it happened. At least I could tell you who was downstairs.'

'I thought you said that your memory was bad.'

'Did I?'

The detectives looked at one another with raised eyebrows. It was apparent that Sheila was as dotty as her husband, with a Miss Marple complex thrown in. She was asked a few innocuous questions and thanked politely, and told that that would be all for the moment.

Sheila was not used to being patronised. If they had had a different attitude she would have told them about the key. She had what she considered to be a photographic memory, and she had spent the morning reviewing the comings and goings she had observed the day before. She was fairly certain that she knew who had killed Corinna, but if the police thought they could work it out for themselves, then let them. She had no need for vengeance. She had long since ceased to view death as a tragedy. In India death was celebrated as a

107

sort of liberation, as a chance to do better in the next reincarnation. Not that she believed in reincarnation, but she knew that she wasn't afraid of her own death, and she didn't like the idea of retribution being taken against anyone who happened to kill her.

'If you're sure that's all,' she said.

'Yes,' they said, 'that's all.' They were anxious to be rid of her, not looking in her direction as if she would go away more easily if they ignored her. By her elbow was the table-load of plastic bags full of Rory's goodies. She had been impressed by the collection. When the idea of taking something first occurred to her, it was to spite the arrogance of the detectives, and it seemed logical to take one of the smaller bags, one they wouldn't notice so easily. She slipped it into her cardigan pocket as she stood up, thinking that it was only a couple of tabs of acid and better to put it to some use than let it waste away in a police vault.

By the time she got out to the oak tree, to the bough which hung over Rory's grave, the acid had not yet taken full effect. She was feeling slightly spongey, but that was all. She noticed that the earth on the grave was flattened in an odd way, and that there was a small hole in the middle of the mound. Perhaps she was imagining it, but she didn't think she was freaking just yet. All the same, it was more than twenty years since her last trip, so she couldn't be sure. She knelt over the little hole to look at it more closely. She sniffed at it. It smelled of earth, and something else. Semen? Was that possible? Now that she looked at it, the hole was about the size of a dick, and the earth was flattened as if a man's body had been flailing over it in an awkward attempt to make love. So Rory had an admirer. She began to laugh at the thought of some frustrated man fucking the grave of her dead son. The image was a sad one, but the laughter was the result of the acid. When the laughter stopped she went a little way off and sat in the wiry grass, to watch the colours change in the sea, and to enjoy her trip.

Jody Comes To

One of the great tragedies of being God is that there is very little mystery in life. There are things, of course, that I don't know. I have no idea what is beyond infinity, and only the haziest system of beliefs to cover the force which created me (I find the modern theories that God is a creation of man very interesting and highly plausible, and would probably believe them were it not for the fact that I got here first). I certainly have no idea what will happen after I have gone. Contrary to popular belief I cannot tell the future. With experience I am becoming a dab hand at forecasting, but I have no crystal balls and, since the date of my birth is unknown, astrology doesn't come into it. Do you think for one moment that if I had had any idea of the future, of this future, that I would have had any truck with the human race at all? Still, given all that, there is less mystery in my life than there is in yours. I don't have to wonder what anyone else is thinking or doing, or worry about who likes me and who would rather see me dead. I know the toadies from the believers and the baddies from the misguided. That could be wonderful, but it isn't. Knowing you as well as I do, there are very few of you worth more than a ball of snot. Not your fault, I admit. You were, after all, created in my image.

There are those who believe in me, and that is really

the saddest thing of all. Countless lives are wasted in my name, praying, abstaining and studying that ridiculous bible thing. That is not what life is for. There will be the whole of eternity to get to grips with theology after you are dead, when you have nothing better to do. Happiness is an elusive quality, I agree, even for the most dedicated of hedonists, but you could at least have a stab at titillating your senses while you've got the chance, while you've got the senses. The trouble is, no, the difference between Rory Dixon and the rest of you is, that most of you get it wrong so easily.

Take our two detectives. Having interviewed Kay and Jody O'Driscoll they left the Commodore Hotel, the wife-beating transvestite-rimming man in front, his companion in his wake. The interviews had not been wholly satisfactory. It was evident that Kay had something to hide, and that it was something that was not necessarily pertinent to the case. Her cautiousness made her a bad witness. Jody was practically autistic in his response to their questions. The detectives agreed that the interviews had been a waste of time.

The first detective we know about. There was no pleasure in his life, only a series of desperate actions which kept total frustration at bay. He hated himself for urges which were, if society were honest, quite normal. Co-existing with this self-hatred was an overbearing egotism, a pride in his masculine middle-class public facet. It is likely that this person will spend his life and die in the trap he has made for himself. He could, of course, be reborn as a Christian, and thereby descend into a worse hell than any he has ever known. As a Christian the poor man would be denied even his harmless weekly visits to Leeson Street.

There is nothing too extraordinary to reveal about the second detective. He lived in a North Dublin suburb with his wife and a small child, played darts on Tuesday night, went to mass every Sunday, and had a low sex drive. I suppose I shouldn't laugh at these people who think that by singing their ghastly hymns they are communicating with me, who gaze in reverence at a middle-aged man with dandruff in a frock and imagine him to be my representative on earth, who look to that pervert in the Vatican for guidance (the dreams that man has about his mother, they even make me blush. I much preferred it when popes had a bit on the side to keep them on the straight and narrow). The second detective goes to mass, not for the usual social reasons, but because he believes. Not only does he believe that he is on the path to eternal life (after a few token years in purgatory for minor misdemeanours which he may have overlooked, such as crossing himself back to front when he wasn't concentrating, or absentmindedly eating a hamburger on Good Friday), but he believes that by venerating the Christian interpretation of my persona he is justifying his existence. He believes, without any encouragement from me, that I love him. And this encompasses his entire miserable life. He had never practised contraception, and would be inundated with children were it not for the pathetically low levels of his testosterone and sperm count. He is driven to trouble his wife only five or six times a year, and these episodes are followed by a decade of the rosary.

Don't you just loathe Christians? The only kick I get out of them is when they meet all the atheists in heaven. I have to have the atheists up here, for a bit of intelligent conversation and for the look on their faces when they meet me. What on earth does it matter whether a mortal believes in me or not? They will find out soon enough. Better to be an atheist and live life like the clappers than to be a handclapping repressed Christian, or a dreary Muslim reeking of mint tea and ox-like certainty, or a poor Hindu so resigned to karma that you will marry any old bat your parents choose, or one of those sanctimonious Jains who wouldn't step in their own shit for fear of injuring a microbe. I used to care. I used to be a great proselytizer, but with the results I've had you can't keep up that sort of guff forever.

The other reason, by the way, that I have the atheists up here is that there isn't anywhere else. There is no hell, or purgatory, or limbo: I lied. I invented all that stuff from the best of motives, but I regret it now. The idea of hell has done more harm than good. Not that everyone gets to heaven. There is a class of people who are excluded, and that, in some ways, is what this document is about. Rory Dixon, whose company I would have preferred to that of any saint, martyr or wit, is one of the excluded. This document is the best I can do to make up for my loss.

Kay O'Driscoll watched from the window on the first floor landing to see that the detectives got into their car and left. Their presence in the hotel had made her feel uneasy. She had lied to them about her relationship with Rory. It was an understandable lie, seeing as her affair with him could have no bearing on the case, but like most people she was intimidated by authority, and would have preferred to face them with a clear conscience. What could be the point of upsetting everyone with self-indulgent confessions now that Rory was dead anyway. On the other hand, now that he was gone, she felt that her own life had slipped away from her also. The things she had valued before his coming – her business, her children, her husband – were not where she had left them when her obsession with Rory began. The business could run itself, her children had no need of her, and her husband was a man she didn't know at all. It was like coming back from holiday to find that your house is full of squatters. She knew that she had to do something to reclaim the rights she had forfeited. She thought she might begin by being honest.

She phoned Helen, but as soon as she announced herself, before she could get another word in, Helen began a distraught near-hysterical monologue, which barely had room in it for polite responses let alone Kay's confession and plea for a new beginning.

Helen said, 'They think I did it. They haven't said anything yet, but they think I did it. Not just Rory, they think I killed Corinna. Sweet Jesus, they must think I am demented. They're working it all out so they can pin it on me. How could they think that? I was the one. I was the only one who said he had been murdered when everyone else said I was mad. How mad can you be? Wouldn't I have let it lie as an accident if I'd done it myself? Kay, you can't believe these men. They sit there sneering at you, treating every innocent remark you make as a confession.'

'I know. They've just been here.'

'There? What were they doing there? What did you tell them? They started asking about my marriage. Did they ask you about my marriage? As if every couple who had a row should check their brake cables in the morning. What did you say?'

'I said you had a healthy marriage, as far as I knew.'

'As far as you knew? Oh, thanks – you might as well have told them I was a homicidal maniac.'

'I said it was a robust marriage.'

'For Christ's sake, Kay, you don't understand. It isn't enough. You have to lie. They are going to put me in prison. Don't speak to them again. Kieran Dunne is coming down from Dublin. I won't speak to them again unless Kieran is there. You too. Insist on a solicitor. I'll send Kieran over. Did they talk to Jody? What did Jody say?'

'Nothing. Jody said nothing. He doesn't these days.'

And so on. The telephone conversation lasted another forty minutes, but Helen was always prone to repetition, so you've got the gist of it. Kay swore as she put the phone down (taking my name in vain as part of the oath, I was interested to see) and went to find her husband.

He was at his desk as usual, playing patience. At

115

first, after the crash, he had spent his time staring into space, but now he had discovered patience, which kept his hands occupied and his mind blank, so blank that he had almost wet himself once or twice without even realising that his bladder was full.

She touched him to make him aware of her presence. Well, she pushed him hard in the shoulder.

'Jody,' she said.

He turned up the ten of diamonds and put it down on the jack of clubs. She took the cards from his hands and swept the cards that were on the desk onto the floor.

'Jody,' she said.

He did look at her, but rather blankly. She had swivelled his chair around so that it faced her.

'This can't go on,' she said.

She slapped his face, as if she was trying to wake him, but he remained slumped in his chair. She undid his trousers and manipulated him to an erection, and then an ejaculation. That was something; that was more response than she had got from him for a long time. He had moaned at the point of coming, and there were streaks of spunk across his shirt front to prove that he was still in the land of the living. She buried her face in the folds of his genitals and wept.

'What was that for?' he said.

'I want you back,' she said.

'Why?'

She had to think about that one. She rubbed his wet foreskin against her nostril and said, 'Because I don't have anything else. Because we used to be in love. Because I can't stand you being like this. Because we are wasting our lives.'

He didn't say anything for a while, and then he said, 'So?' But he had put his hand to her shirt, and he was stroking her nipple with his thumb, curiously, as if he knew nothing about nipples, as if this nipple hadn't

116

been part of his life for half of his lifetime.

'I still love you,' she said.

'So?'

'I think this is because you know.'

'Know what?'

'Know something. I want to tell you anyway. I think you know already, and if I tell you the air will be clear. And even if you don't know already, it's better if you do. Anything is better than this.'

She was looking hard at his face, searching for a reaction, for a clue about where she should begin, but his face showed nothing except that he was watching his own thumb move against her nipple, telling it backwards and forwards like a prayer bead.

She said, 'Rory and I were lovers.' She stopped for his reaction which was, in fact, a little smile.

'You knew,' she said.

He shook his head.

She said, 'That's about it, really. It went on for ten years. He kept me sane and he drove me mad. I never felt guilty about it. I still don't. I'm not telling you out of guilt. I'm telling you so that we have a chance to get on with the rest of our lives. I don't think I was in love with him. I did it for pleasure. With him pleasure was distilled into a pure form. It wasn't anything he did, or technique, or anything he said. It was just that he enjoyed it so much. If somebody enjoys you to that degree, it can get addictive. It was always worth the risk, whatever it was I was risking. I should have felt bad about you, because you were so fond of him, and if you had found out, you would have been hurt by the betrayal. But it never seemed likely that you would find out, not with Rory's luck. Maybe you knew all the time. I sometimes thought that you did know, that you and Rory talked about it. I wouldn't have put it past Rory, but I don't think that you would have been capable of it. You aren't good at deceit. That was

117

one of the reasons I fell in love with you in the first place. And maybe I have another reason for telling you. Maybe I'm being cruel. Because of what his death has done to you. Maybe if you knew that he wasn't such a good friend, that he did betray you, maybe if you knew that, this grief would stop. But I don't want that either. I liked the way you were fond of Rory. I'm jealous of how badly you've taken his death. I wish I had half the feeling in me that you have. Rory never said anything bad about you. Nor I when I was with him. In spite of what we were doing, the two of us loved you. Sometimes, it was as though you were a part of it. He was good. He was very good.'

Jody said, 'I know.'

She waited a long time for him to say something else. He moved her head, and at the sight of his own genitals, laughed. Not an outright laugh, more a smiling exhalation, and he began to put himself away and do his trousers up.

'What now?' she said. 'Aren't you angry? Be angry. Be something. Don't shut yourself off from me again. Do you understand?'

'Yes,' he said. 'I know why now. I always thought it was only a matter of chance. I always thought it had something to do with me, but he came for illicit sex, and he wasn't a man to be thwarted.'

She would have liked to ask him to explain himself, but even if he was talking nonsense, the fact that he was talking to her at all was something. She was prepared to put off comprehension until a later date, so long as there was some communication in the interim.

What he was talking about, what he was thinking of, was an event which she could never have imagined, though it would be no great surprise to her once she knew of it. He was thinking about a day, three years previously, in the middle of winter, when Rory had come calling at the Commodore Hotel.

There was nothing fantastically unusual in an

unexpected visit from Rory, but this one was slightly awkward, and had Jody been a man with a more suspicious nature he would have seen why. In the first place it was one of his lecture days and he should, under normal circumstances, have been in Dublin. But the students' union had called a strike and the college had phoned him to tell him that he might as well stay at home. And in the second place Kay would have been there, but her mother had had a stroke and she had gone haring off to Dungarvan. It was plain now that Rory and Kay had planned an assignation, and that was why, having bounded in the back door of the house, Rory had recoiled slightly at the sight of Jody. But it was only a momentary, barely perceptible awkwardness. And if Rory had seemed slightly off-balance for the duration of their conversation, that could have been explained by what happened towards the end of it.

It must have been inevitable, because the reason Rory put his arms around Jody in the first place was that Jody had begun to shake. All right, they had had a few drinks, and fine, they were doing one of those soul-piercing conversations that Rory was so expert at, and when Rory put his arms around the other man it seemed like the most natural thing in the world, and Jody was more grateful than anything.

Then in a hoarse whisper Rory said, 'Jody, take your clothes off.'

It might not seem like the most spellbinding of seduction lines, but coming from a seemingly heterosexual man for whom you have craved in an unspecified way over the years, given a gap that wide between desire and expectation, there was no possibility of disobedience. When Rory nipped out to the kitchen to fetch a bottle of olive oil Jody did worry slightly about which end things were to be taken from, but he should have known that Rory would be as generous in bed as he had been in friendship.

Until now, in the light of Kay's confession, he had

119

never quite understood how or why it had started. He and Rory became regular, though not frequent, lovers. They would slip off, as though for a toot, in the middle of parties and make love in a field, or sometimes they would do it in the spare bedroom at Innish, where Rory kept a supply of K-Y in the third drawer down of the bedside table, the key of which had reputedly been lost years before. Jody never questioned the smoothness of Rory's arrangements. He assumed that he had had predecessors, but liked to think that, apart from Helen, he had no contemporaries. That was a testament to Rory's talent for making you feel that you were the only person that mattered.

There are people who, given Jody's position, would follow up their wife's confession with a confession of their own. Perhaps truth is infectious. Perhaps sinners are prone to one-upmanship. And Jody might have done so, but he had lost any talent he ever had for speaking to his wife.

She said, the way people will, even though they know it is the worst possible thing to say, 'What are you thinking?'

'Leave me alone,' he said. 'I want to be left with my own memories of him. You aren't the only one with memories and no regrets.'

And that was when he saw the joke of it all, and began to laugh, and that was something she really couldn't bear, because genuine laughter will override the most cherished tragedy. Given a choice, she, like most, would choose the tragic before the ridiculous.

I too was laughing, but not at them. At that moment that second detective was crossing himself as he was being driven past the church in Hoareswood, out of respect.

Witnesses

The summer was behaving beautifully. There were nights of rain and days of blazing heat. There was a constant coming and going of neatly-grilled and thirsty tourists through the Commodore Hotel. Kay even considered asking Jody if he would help out in the bar, as he had sometimes done in the past, on sufferance. She wondered if it would be good for him to have to deal with people, but by the time she had resolved to ask, she couldn't find him.

Their conversation had had some effect on him. It had brought him out of apathy and made him restless. For ten minutes after she had left him to go and count the lobsters for the evening, he paced the room, overtaken with anxieties. For the first time since Rory's death he wanted to think, to restore the order of his once well-ordered mind, if only to remind himself what it had been like to be the person he was before, and to see if that was any more worthwhile than being the person he had become since. Things were going badly wrong. It was perhaps right that Rory should have died, since he had stretched his life to the limits of possibility, and death had saved him from the decline that would come with old age. But Corinna was a different matter. There was a child who had been so trapped in her own misery that she had never had the chance to live at all. What was worse was the smallness of the effect of her

121

death. Of course it had been a great scandal, but only because it had thrown new light on Rory's death, only because it had taken place in the presence of so many eminent people, only because it involved the sort of detail that the newspapers liked to print. There was no mention of anyone's loss; there was nothing to suggest that her dying might have been a loss to herself.

Jody had not stepped outside the building for nine days. Now, for the first time, he felt trapped in it. At any moment Kay could return to the study. He dreaded that. His defences against her were gone, and he hadn't yet worked out what to say to her when the time came to speak. He needed to go somewhere where he wouldn't be disturbed, for a few hours at least. If the tide was out he could go for a long walk along the shoreline, perhaps even as far as the Black Rock. He left his study like a sneak thief and made his way down one of the back stairs, the one that was known as the Devil's staircase, where the ghosts of Crutchet friars were said to perambulate on the seventh of every month. It was the sort of house that attracted ghost stories. The dourness and the greyness of the building worked on the imagination, particularly at night when it was caught in the sweep of the Hook Lighthouse; when, apart from the lighthouse itself, it was the only perpendicular object on the flattened landscape of that part of the peninsula. Even on a summer's day, when knots of resting windsurfers and Pimms' drinkers gathered on the terraces, the building itself was forbidding, constructed during a period in the nineteenth century when romance was identified with *mementi mori* and houses were made to look like large tombs.

Unaccustomed to the glare of the midday sun, Jody made his way to the stone pier, which was unoccupied save for a figure in black who sat on a bollard. He could see that it was a priest, but there was something exaggerated about him. He looked too much like a priest, like a method actor who has studied all the elements of priestliness and was giving a performance too intense to be realistic. If Jody had believed in the ghosts of the Commodore Hotel, he might have been forgiven for thinking that this man was one of them.

It was in fact Father Cooper, the funeral orator. Had it been a mere mortal, Jody would have ignored him. But he had been raised to have respect for the cloth and, although religion had long since ceased to be of any importance to him, he felt an obligation to be polite. In any case, the tide was in and there was no possibility of taking the walk he had planned. He might as well allow this man to talk to him until he had thought of an alternative.

They greeted, and muttered the usual remarks about the seascape and the day. Then the priest said, 'I came to bury a friend. You might have known him?'

Jody made no answer, though he knew that it must be Rory the priest was talking of. Half the guests in the hotel had come to bury him.

The priest said, 'Rory Dixon?'

'I knew him.'

The priest said, 'I didn't see you at the funeral.'

'No.' The accusation caused some resentment in Jody.

'It was a great turnout. But I'd know if I'd seen you.'

Jody did his best to look unimpressed by this demonstration of priestly omnipotence. The beady eye that counts the absences in the largest of congregations. Never mind who turns up; it's the sinners we want. That overblown parable of the shepherd risking his entire flock to brainwash the one ewe with a streak of individuality.

'Terrible business,' the priest said. 'A young girl like that. To be driven to patricide and suicide. God rest her soul.'

Perhaps the heartfelt platitudes irritated Jody. He sounded half-angry when he said, 'She didn't kill him.'

123

'Oh, I know. That's what they're saying now. They have all sorts of theories. The place is full of amateur detectives. Journalists. We're all under suspicion now. The lot of us. I was questioned myself this morning, by the real thing. Dublin men. I don't know why. The case is as plain as it is straightforward. But I suppose they have to be sure.'

'She didn't kill him.'

'And how would you know that?'

Jody hadn't meant to say anything to this man, or to anyone else. But the priest's complacency was goading him. And there was something deep in his nurturing which made it acceptable to confess before a man in a dog collar. He said, 'I was there. I saw him die. I was with him the morning he died. I know who and I know why and I know how.'

When his voice stopped he realised that he had sounded petulant, and it seemed appropriate that the priest should patronise him by saying, 'Is that a fact?'

Jody thought how ridiculous the other man seemed, with his uniform and his dandruff, and a prim mouth that was used only for nutrition and speech, and his long white hands joined together between his knees, and the hair that sprouted from his nose as an orchestrated testament to the absence of vanity in him, and the ease with which it was possible to predict his next utterance.

'I suppose you told the police?'

Jody almost said, 'It's for me to know and them to find out.' The company of this man was making him regress to a childhood state, back to the point where he had left off worrying about religion and resenting priests, and feeling guilty about his dissimulations in the confessional. He had a debt of resentment to pay back to this man, who represented a profession which had been responsible for all the worst miseries of his early years.

The priest made an adroit change of subject. 'You knew Rory well then?'

'Better than you.' The bitter answers seemed to be coming out of their own accord.

'Maybe. I wouldn't be able to say that for sure. I knew the man a long time back. We grew up together on the same mountain, and we walked across it to the same school. I never forgot him. But then, his name was in the papers often enough. He was a great success.'

'He was a good fuck, too.' Perhaps that was an attempt on Jody's part to end the conversation, to leave the priest speechless and defeated. The word itself, let alone the act described, should have had the same effect on this man as a crucifix on a vampire.

But the priest was nonplussed, and said, 'So you knew him as well as that? I had a feeling he might go on as he started. We're all only human, and he knew that better than anyone.'

There was some sort of metamorphosis in progress. The priest sat on his bollard in a different way; he crossed his legs; he pushed his hand through his hair, touching the scalp at the back of his head with an unclerical sensuality; his face lost its *I understand you and forgive you* demeanour.

'I suppose,' he said, 'you've been straight with me, so I may as well be straight with you. Just between ourselves. This is all my eye. I lost the right to wear this clobber a long time ago. It was a joke. No trivial joke. It was a joke made in earnest. I was a priest once, but they soon rumbled. I suppose that was Rory's influence. How could you have seen the world through that man's eyes and go on to take Maynooth College seriously? After I preached my first sermon they sent me off to the missions. The theory was that the savages didn't know enough English to absorb the subtleties of my blasphemy. Anyway, it's a long story but I was kicked out in the end. I'm an actor now, most of the time. I do kitchen sink parodies at the Edinburgh fringe. I thought the one last thing I could do for Rory was to see him safely into the ground; to save him being buried by the parish crow. But then the girl got killed, and I'm stuck here. If the cops try to check up on me I'm bollixed.'

Jody's head was reeling. 'Fuck you,' he said.

The priest laughed. 'Well, you can if you like. You wouldn't be the first. That was Rory himself. Me, along with half the girls and boys over three parishes and half a mountain. Those were the days. Where are you going?'

Jody had walked to the end of the pier. He wanted to go where this creature on the bollard couldn't follow him. The man was a ghoul. Any moment now, Jody felt, he would lift his cassock and expose himself, exploiting the intimacy which had been forced between them. Jody's best hope was that the small boat would be tied in its usual place at the bottom of the steps. If it wasn't, he would take his shoes off and swim for it.

The boat was there, oars and all. It was kept for the use of guests who were fond of fishing, and had probably been booked for the afternoon, but Jody's need was greater. He had untied the boat and pushed it away from the steps before the priest got to the end of the pier. Unfortunately, to row away he would have to face the other man, but he kept his head bent to the oars and his ears deaf to the shouts, and pulled long strokes until he was breathless and out of range.

When he looked up, the priest was standing at the end of the pier, skimming stones after him. He was too far away to make his expression out clearly, but he seemed to be laughing, his arm swinging with each cast of a pebble, and the stones skipping over the water and sinking, midway between the boat and the land.

Jody rowed on, with less exertion, up the estuary on the brimming tide, Hook and Crook before him and the weight of the river behind him, the blasting heat of the sun on his face and his hands. It was an easy boat, designed to be handled by the most incompetent of holiday amateurs. There were bad currents that would sweep you out into the Atlantic, but they were easy to avoid once you were aware of them. In forty-five minutes he was level with the Black Rock, and he let the boat drift for a while as he surveyed the pinnacle which had held the blue Spider, and found the spot on the headland from where he had watched it happen. Whatever enlightenment he was expecting from that view, it never occurred to him, and he rowed on. He wasn't fit but he was strong, and there was no fat on his body to impede him. After an initial tiredness he got into the swing of it, thinking of the recent discovery that galley slaves in the ancient world were given the seeds of *Cannabis sativa* to chew on while they rowed, that the world economy had been fuelled by hashish in the time of Christ, and sniggering to think of St Paul in manacles, stoned out of his tiny.

This, out on the estuary, was a form of freedom. He felt a bizarre elation, at odds with the experiences which had so far circumscribed his day. He had escaped from Kay, and then from the priest, and until the prow of the boat should hit a beach he was his own man. He might have guessed that his state was nearer to hysteria than to happiness, but for the moment he was enjoying it. He sang, loudly and out of tune, Fux's version of the song of Orpheus on finding Eurydice. The Commodore Hotel was a grey rectangle in the distance and the beach at Innish was rising up behind him. He waved to distant people lounging on distant strands.

Sheila was coming down from her trip as his boat approached, but she kept her place, sitting on the spot where she had been since morning. She had had a good, gentle time. Perhaps they didn't make acid as strong as they used to, or perhaps the acid she had

127

taken had been lying around for too long and lost some of its kick. In either case, it was just as well. It had given her a feeling of well-being and great comfort. She was almost optimistic about facing an evening with her batty daughter-in-law and her senescent husband. She watched Jody beach his boat and climb the crumbling slope, and wondered if this had been the man who had visited the grave the night before and left his deposit in the mound, and then wondered if that had been something she had really seen or something which she had hallucinated.

He looked very young in the distance, walking with that adolescent gait that has no fear of falling but which has an element of timidity all the same. Close to he seemed older, but still boyish for a man of middle age. He was dark and not extraordinary or offensive to look at. A little bit fogeyish perhaps, but in a harmless way, as though he could still grow out of it. He looked like one of those pipe-smoking well-jawed men from advertisements in the fifties, one of those carelessly immaculate men who always seem to have clean fingernails yet never seem to wash their hands. Having thought this, she looked at his fingernails first when he was near enough. They were bitten down so badly that there was no room for dirt in them. She didn't like his hands. There was something overly intimate about them, as if it would not be taken amiss if you grabbed hold of one of them. So her thoughts babbled on, while she was only half-aware that the drug was still at work in her.

'Where did you come from?' she said.

'Over there.' He pointed towards the Commodore.

'The big place?'

'Yes.'

'What is it?'

'It's where I live.'

They could have gone on with this semi-conversation

forever, but he spotted the mound beneath the oak tree.

'Is that where they buried him?' he said.

'It wasn't you so.'

'It wasn't me what?'

'Give me a pull up and I'll show you.'

He offered her his hand and hauled her to her feet, surprised by her being so tall once she got there. She kept hold of his hand and led him to the grave, thinking that she had been right about those hands: they were an invitation to be held. She pointed out the desecration to him.

'Well,' he said. 'I suppose these things happen.'

'Not where I come from,' she said.

He looked at her for a few seconds, realising who she was. 'You're his mother,' he said.

'And you are?'

'No one. A friend. Jody O'Driscoll.'

'In that order?'

He smiled at her joke.

Then she said, 'I know who you are. You are the one who was hard taken. I met your wife. She brought food. I don't suppose, seeing the way you came, that you wanted to find anyone here. I'll go if you like.'

'No,' he said. 'You have more right to it than I have.' He bent down beside the mound suddenly and put his finger to the soil. 'Fish,' he said.

'What?'

'That's a fish scale.'

'So it is.'

'Are you all right?' he said. She was looking a bit swoony.

'Yes,' she said. 'It's just, the fish thing is freaking me a bit.'

'Oh. Rory said once that you were a guru, or a goddess or something.'

'Is that right,' she said. 'And what did that make him?'

129

'You tell me. Was there a bit of parthenogenesis involved by any chance?'

'Not likely,' she said, and turned to her good side and gave him the glad eye. A bit of flirtation was making her feel herself again. They had begun, by an unspoken consent, to walk back towards the house, slowly and by an indirect route.

'I'm sorry about Corinna,' he said.

She thanked him, and then said, 'Do you know, you're the first person to say that? The girl might as well have been the Christmas turkey for all the effect her death has had around here.'

'Helen?' he said. She said nothing, so he continued, 'Helen isn't as bad as she seems. She was too dependent on Rory, and she didn't get on with Corinna. She hasn't it in her to encompass two deaths so close to each other. If it had only been Corinna who died, she'd be in a bad way about it. There'd be a lot of guilt. She won't get around to that until she's over Rory. And she may never be. You can't condemn her for not suffering. Suffering is nearly all she does.'

'You aren't as gormless as you look,' she said.

They had come to the top of the rise, from where they could see down to the house. There was a squad car in the drive, and another leaving.

'They should leave the dead to themselves,' she said. 'Not all this poking and prodding. What for? It's only a game of find-the-killer. Nobody here is crying out for blood and revenge, except Helen. And the way things are going they think she's the one who did it.'

'Which? Rory or Corinna?'

'Both, I suppose. I assumed it was the same man did both.'

'It couldn't be,' he said, without thinking. They had both stopped walking, each realising that the other knew something. Sheila had pronounced the word man with a conviction which gave it a narrower meaning than the generic. Jody had contradicted her with the impatience of one who is not merely theorising. They hesitated before embarking on an inevitable exchange of information.

Then Jody said, 'Man?'

'I don't know why I bother,' she said. 'I tried to tell those other two. Smig and Smug. The two detectives. At the time I thought they dismissed me because they thought I was senile. Would you think, to look at me, that I was senile?'

Jody laughed at her.

'It isn't funny. Well, anyway, I can see now that they haven't the slightest interest in what happened. They are looking for the neatest tidiest solution, preferably without a trial at the end of it. If they could get a verdict of suicide on Corinna, they would. But they won't. The next best thing they can do is go after Helen. She's half-mad anyway. It would be the easiest thing in the world to lock her up in an asylum.'

'Are you saying that you know?' he said.

'Are you?' She was almost enjoying this game of you-show-me-yours-and-I'll-show-you mine.

'I don't know who killed Corinna.'

'But you know who killed Rory. Fair enough. I suppose you have your reasons for keeping it to yourself.'

'I did,' he said. 'I'm not sure that reason comes into it anymore. While his death was an accident. That seemed the best thing all round. For his sake as much as anyone's.'

'So you didn't kill him yourself?'

'Who knows?' he said. 'Who can say that the passive aren't as culpable as anyone?'

'Do you want a job running an ashram?' she said. 'You seem to know the basics already. It's only a matter of telling people what they already know in a language they have been too stupid to learn for themselves. You'd look good in a lungi.'

He was thinking too gravely to respond to her flattery. 'Are you serious?' he said. 'They're going to frame Helen?'

'Why?' she said. 'What are you going to do about it?'

'I don't know. Tell them the truth, if it came to it.'

'Would they believe you? And if they did, wouldn't they just pin it on you instead? Look, there's more going on here than the odd killing.'

'What, for instance?'

'How would I know? Do you want to find out? We could have a lash at it. Maybe I had enough of being the wise old woman in the jungle. I did sometimes think that if I met another German hippy on the road to nirvana I'd stuff his chappals down his throat and send him back to Krupps to get himself a decent job. There's no soot being a guru. Anyone worth the trouble knows it all already.'

'Who'll be Holmes and who'll be Watson?'

'Bagsy I Holmes,' she said. 'He was the one who got to snort all the coke.'

The Long Arm of the Law

Alan Kehoe did not fish the day following the
funeral. Moby waited an hour for him on the boat
and then went up to the house to see if he had over-
slept, but he hadn't been seen since the night before,
when he had come back from Innish. He had taken off
his good clothes and they were laid across his bed,
which hadn't been slept in. His fishing clothes were
missing. His mother had heard him leave the house in
the early hours, but she had assumed that he and Moby
were making an early start to make up for the day lost
at the funeral.

'He must be off somewhere,' she said. 'I suppose
he's upset.'

'I'll give him upset,' Moby said, with a bravado that
he knew Doreen Kehoe wouldn't challenge.

'Wasn't it terrible about the girl?' she said. 'And he
saw the whole thing. He probably couldn't sleep and
had to walk it off. He'll be waiting for you down at the
boat when you get back.'

Moby snorted. He was cross with Alan because there
was work to be done, but now his crossness was mitigated by the company of Doreen in her night attire.
He desired every inch of her, from the purple nylon
fluff of her slippers up to the clips in her flattened hair.
Being with child had brought a bloom to her and she
looked younger, closer to the thirty-two she was than

133

the forty she acted. Her life so far had not been wonderful: pregnant at fifteen by a passing stranger, she had scraped a living since with menial work and social security. She cleaned the rooms at the Commodore Hotel, getting there and back by bicycle. Once she had tried training as a hairdresser, but that was the year that Alan had tuberculosis, so she had to give it up. And as a girl with a reputation, hers was the house that drunken men came knocking and bawling at after the pubs shut. If Moby had his way all that would be put behind her now.

'Have you decided yet?' he said.

'You shouldn't be asking,' she said. 'Give me time. I told you I wanted to. It's only Alan. He'll come round to it soon enough.'

'You don't want to be going to the altar when you're eight months gone. Alan may as well do his coming round to it after as before.'

He would have liked to use Alan's absence as an excuse to spend the morning with her, but the fishing had to come first or there'd be no money for a wedding in any case. He could manage on his own for the day. He took his leave of her.

'He'll be down at the boat,' she said. 'You'll see.'

But Alan wasn't at the boat, and Moby set out alone, cursing the boy for being the chief blight on his pursuit of happiness. It was a consolation that Alan was getting to the age when he would be leaving home soon. Then he and Doreen could have a chance of a life together, with the new baby and any more that came along. Moby had been a bachelor for long enough to imagine that family life was an idyll. In the thirty years since his own mother had died he had forgotten all the strains and tensions, and could only remember the security of a warm kitchen and the smell of frying rashers of bacon.

It had still been dark when Alan had left the house that morning. It was his intention, as his mother rightly

134

guessed, only to walk for a bit to clear his head, in the absence of the possibility of sleep. The rain of the night had lessened to a fine drizzle, and he took the hill that rose out of the village and curled over the headlands and dips of the estuary coastline. He was walking, he knew, in the direction of Innish, but he thought no more of it than that. Innish was beyond what was counted as walking distance. All the same, he knew that he was being drawn towards the place. Innish was the source of his disturbance. He couldn't sleep because he knew that every time he closed his eyes he would see Corinna's body in the bath, with the gash across her neck and her bloodless skin the texture of white rubber. And Innish was where Rory Dixon's body was planted in the ground, the body that had begun this nightmare.

He walked until his legs became so heavy that it seemed they were beyond his control, and then he watched the black shadows they made as they swung forwards, one after the other, like lead pendulums from his waist. Then he knew, if tiredness wouldn't stop him, he was going to Innish.

He arrived in a grey and yellow dawn and made his way to the graveside. The drizzle had stopped, and the sea was changing colour like a cheap hologram. Beneath the leaves of the oak tree, despite the drips that fell, the ground was still reasonably dry, the black soil on the grave flattened by the backs of shovels. Alan sat with his head in his knees and wept. He wept because exhaustion had weakened him to a point where he couldn't not weep, and he loathed his own weeping and would have done anything to make his eyes dry again. He was out of control.

He fucked Rory Dixon's grave out of anger, as much as an insult to the dead as a testimonial to the erotic power of the dead man. And his anger, like all anger, had grown out of his fear. And his fear had grown out of the day he had pulled Rory from the blue Spider:

135

his mother's betrayal and his arousal in the water and his tryst with the murdered girl on the wall by the river. When he had spilled his seed into the black ground he ran away, as the shadows of daylight were forming across the grass.

He spent the morning watching crabs and sea anemones in the rock pools along the shoreline, until hunger and the rising tide brought him back into the real world at midday.

He was the only customer in the pub at Priesthaggard, and the barman thought of questioning his age, but since he only asked for a cup of tea and a ham sandwich there was no harm in it. The barman, of course, only wanted to talk about the goings-on at Innish. Alan listened to him, pretending to know nothing about it, until the barman mentioned that he knew Aidan Connelly, implying thereby that he had inside information. He said that Aidan had been given a week's leave, which was a sure sign that there was trouble brewing.

Alan had a very clear picture of Aidan's face from their meeting in Ballinglass, the day the body had been found. He could see the big ears and the crossed teeth as if Aidan were standing before him, and he had a vague memory of Aidan saying that if Alan had any more information, he would be interested to know. Alan wasn't sure that he had any information at all, but he badly wanted to talk to someone, and Aidan's was the only face he had seen in the last few weeks that seemed a possible recipient of anything he might have to say. As casually as he could, he asked the barman where Aidan lived, trying to make his curiosity seem no more than the habitual nosiness of the countryside. Then he let the conversation drift on for another quarter of an hour or so before asking for the phone book.

Their meeting, while not exactly furtive, had the air

of something clandestine to it. Aidan had been warned by the sergeant that this was a time for keeping his head low, until the Dixon thing had washed over them and the men from Dublin had finished the work they had been set. The sergeant didn't say it in so many words, but the implication was that the job given to the Dublin detectives had been one of creative obfuscation, that there was no danger of anything so impertinent as the truth emerging. Aidan had no real choice but to comply with all this, even though he was young enough to have a conscience and his conscience was made uneasy by it. He would have liked to see himself in the rôle of a heroic fifth columnist, unearthing the facts that would bring the great and the bad to justice, but he had no idea where to begin. So he took his week's leave and prepared to spend his afternoons watching motor racing on the television. He had only just switched the set on when the phone rang.

He arranged to pick Alan up at the petrol pumps outside the pub. As he drove to the rendezvous, he did nothing to suppress the cops-and-robbers thrill he felt. This was more like it; at last, a chance for some excitement. He had never had any illusions that being a policeman would be a life of televisual adventure, but he had expected a bit more than the pedestrian nature of his lot so far, more than being chauffeur to the fat sergeant and checking up on shotgun licences and directing tourists to the nearest bed and breakfast. As he drove he speculated, and as he speculated he grew more excited. What could Alan Kehoe have to tell him? That he had seen Corinna on the clifftop with a pair of pliers in her hand? Or perhaps it was something to do with Corinna's death. Perhaps the girl hadn't committed suicide, and Alan knew who had done it, or better still wanted to confess to having done it himself. Aidan Connelly indulged himself with these fantasies until he rounded a bend and saw the form of the fisherboy by the pumps, and remembered that reality was more intractable than that. The way the boy stood, the shape into which his body had gathered, was an abstract representation of fear and anger. The last thing that Alan resembled was a witness who was about to confess a flood of useful information. He looked as though he would have to hit someone a clatter in the teeth before he might be able to express his first syllable.

The boy got into the car and nothing was said. Aidan drove to the Ballyhack ferry and they crossed into the next county. Other passengers on the ferry left their cars and stood at the railing in the sunshine, taking photographs and pointing out fishing boats to each other like children in sunglasses, but our two didn't even roll their windows down, each of them overtaken with doubt and wondering what on earth the meeting was in aid of in the first place, and which of them was going to speak.

Halfway across the estuary Aidan spoke. He said, 'Well?'

They were safely out of one county and not quite in the next one. They could go to a small pub where neither of them would be known, or drive the back roads as if they were looking for scenery. It was the time to begin talking.

Alan looked around him at the men and women in shorts and the women with painted fingernails who were off to Waterford for an afternoon's shopping, and he wondered for the first time what it was that made the difference between him and the rest of humanity. It seemed that the world was full of people with money and cars and straightforward sex-lives and the ability to talk to strangers, people who didn't have to look at the cadavers of the girls to whom they had lost their virginity, and who would never in a million years desecrate the grave of an architect without at least having a tangible motive. He would have given anything to know the secret formula of normality. Ten days before he had considered himself normal, but he could see now that that had been a false presumption, because he hadn't been happy. He had never, as far as he could remember, been happy. Often in the middle of laughter he would feel himself withdrawing from his laughing body, and he would watch it, thinking how foolish it looked, and thinking that nothing was that funny, that the laughter was a kind of virus he had caught from the person he was laughing with, that it would pass in a few seconds. As the ferry hit the concrete slipway at Passage East and he watched two girls of about his own age, laughing, get into the back of their parents' car, he said, 'I don't know.'

Aidan said, 'Neither do I. I was hoping you'd tell me.'

Alan racked his brain for something concrete to tell this man. The day's newspapers had been spread across the bar in Priesthaggard, and he had read the stories with half an eye while the barman was talking to him. He knew that they couldn't be true, but had to think hard to work out the discrepancies between them and the slim facts he was aware of. He knew that Aidan had not met him to hear a self-pitying litany of adolescent confusion. That much was a relief. The things he most needed to talk about were things that he knew he would never mention to anyone. It crossed his mind, now that they were on the open road with nothing but hedges and seascape to look at, that perhaps his experiences of the last week were not uncommon, that everyone, even the people in sunglasses on the ferry, was capable of the same, but that no one ever spoke of it. He would be safe as long as he kept it to himself. He didn't necessarily find this theory credible, but the possibility cheered him up for the moment and he concentrated on finding something to say that Aidan would want to hear, something that would justify this cloak-and-dagger car drive. He could start with the rumours he had heard in the last week, things that were being said and believed by half the people he met. It was possible that Aidan knew them already, but they were not the sort of things that most people would risk saying in the company of a policeman.

'The story is,' he said, 'that it was the boys did Dixon in.'

'The boys?'

'Yeah. The story is he was putting a building up in the North somewhere and the boys were in on it and he crossed them.'

Aidan swore. This was not the sort of thing that he wanted to hear. It was one thing to pull the rug out from under Sergeant Foley. The only thing at risk there was a career that he had doubts about in any case. It was a different matter entirely to be tangling with the boys, where the best you could hope for was a shattered kneecap. If the boys were in on it, that would explain Foley's reluctance to ask questions. Perhaps the men from Dublin were Special Branch, sent to keep things under wraps here while bigger fish were being fried elsewhere.

'And Corinna,' Alan said. 'She didn't top herself. Anyone could have seen that. I know there was a note and everything.'

'Why?'

'She was left-handed. Her left hand was hanging over the side of the bath and there was no blood on it. If she'd cut her own throat there would have been blood on her fingers.'

'How do you know that?'

'I was there.'

'I know you were there. I mean, how do you know she was left-handed? I didn't know you knew her.'

What could he answer? Could he say that he remembered every second and every movement of her body

140

on the wall by the river, that he could remember one of her hands being more efficient than the other in the manipulation of his penis?

'I just know,' he said. 'You don't have to believe me. Ask anyone who knew her better.'

'Did you know her or not?'

'I talked to her, yeah.'

'When?'

'Just before she went into the bathroom.'

'About what?'

'Nothin'. It was only talk. I liked her.'

Aidan heard an echo in that of something the boy had said before, the day in Ballinglass. He had said that he liked Dixon, based entirely on a posthumous relationship. Now he was saying that he knew Corinna to be left-handed, after a chat at the bathroom door. Was he claiming to be psychic or what? It was plain that there was no point in asking him to explain himself.

'Is there anything else?' Aidan said.

'I don't think so, no.'

'We may as well head back so.'

Aidan slowed the car until they were alongside a gateway where he turned it. While it was half across the road Alan said, 'That's OK. You can drop me here. I'll get out.'

'What? Here?'

They were on high ground over the estuary, from where you could pick out all the landmarks: the lighthouse, the hotel, the Black Rock, the beach at Innish, the Martello tower above Ballinglass. You could follow the change in the landscape where it turned from battered coast to rich farmland. If you had field glasses you would have been able to see that the black dot out on the water was a lone man rowing up the coast. A telescope would have shown it to be Jody O'Driscoll. It was odd to see your own half of the world from the other side.

141

Alan had opened the door and was getting out. 'I was going to Waterford anyway,' he said. It was a lie, but he was desperate to do something to cut short his time in the car, and if they crossed the river again he didn't know where he could go. Home to his mother? To artless questions and sympathy, and maybe Moby calling round in the evening. To Gavinstown? To Denny Power's, haunted with memories of Corinna, or at least with memories of his brief obsession with her. He felt better this side of the river, and he had a few pounds in his pocket. Waterford would be his next stop and after that anywhere would do, so long as no one knew who he was.

'Come back,' Aidan said. 'Get in. Let me drop you in Waterford, at least.'

'That's all right,' he said. 'I'll hitch.'

He was already walking away up the road between the thick clouds of meadowsweet. When Aidan thought about it afterwards in the years to follow, he knew for a second, from the way the boy was walking, that he wouldn't be seen again. But hindsight and guilt are a strong combination. Maybe all he felt in reality was relief at the end of a difficult meeting. And he knew too that he would do nothing about what Alan had told him. It wasn't that he was frightened, but his common sense told him that if he interfered he might have cause to be very frightened indeed.

Parallel to him, on a not dissimilar road on the other side of the Barrow, between one token interview and the next, the two detectives were having a sullen argument in their car. The second Godfearing detective had been slow to realise what was happening, but at last an inkling had filtered through his mind. He had begun to suspect that their function in this part of the country was not to solve a crime. The other one of course denied it and he could have pacified his colleague had he been more tactful, but he had reacted badly to the

142

stupidity and the naivety of the other. There was a job to be done for which they were paid. If they had been told to gather certain facts – not to come to any conclusions, but merely to present the right facts in the right order to their superiors – what business was it of theirs? He had had misgivings about taking this man along with him, but the theory from on high had been that the fewer who knew what was going on the better. And an enthusiastic innocent on the case wouldn't necessarily be an encumbrance; indeed, might be an advantage if enquiries were ever made. But now the second detective was going to make things difficult.

He was sulking. He hadn't raised objections with a view to a fight. All he had required was that his conscience be sedated back into its normal condition. The last thing he wanted was for there to be some substance to his misgivings. A complication like that might be the end of him. He believed, despite any evidence to the contrary, that his job was being done for the general good, much as he believed in the goodness of the Church. With the voice of a young boy whose feelings have been hurt he began to back down before the impatience of the other man, and had begun a sentence with the words 'I didn't think' when he was interrupted.

'We aren't fucking paid to think.' The first detective said that in all seriousness, and it was accepted without question by his colleague. It made an end to the argument and they were able to carry on to their destination: in an uneasy silence perhaps, but with the moral issue settled to the satisfaction of both of them.

Architecture and Morality

L ove wouldn't be as bad as this. So what the fuck is love anyway, if this is as good as it gets? I was the first to get into the love thing, before the Romantics, before the Roman de la Rose, before the Song of Solomon and before the Epic of Gilgamesh. When all you had was instinct and a hunger between your legs, I was already a hardened victim, a softened epicure; I suppose what I was saying is, I was the first to be lonely.

And wishful-thinking Christians will tell you that God is love, as if the disease of love had overtaken me, as if I were a heart-shaped satin-cushioned box of chocolates, as if it could be forgotten that I was once called the Scourge of the Nations, as if LOVE were not written over the Inquisition as FREEDOM was written over the camps, as if the simplicity which can be found in nothing else can be invested in me. Heaven has been made so celluloid, so unbelievable, that all it needs now is a double-page spread in *Hello!* magazine.

And if not love, then what? There was a time when I thought I knew and it seemed that there was a masterplan. There was a time when I was patient and took the trouble to explain, like some sort of third-rate evangelist who believes that he knows the meaning of life; I used to feel an obligation to put their minds at rest once they had survived their lives on earth and gained paradise. But to tell the truth, if I ever did know I've forgotten now. And it isn't just senility. The things you forget are the things that never impinged on you in the first place.

This legendary land where Rory Dixon was spawned, the little piece of heaven which fell from the sky and was populated by the lost tribe of Israel who lived underground, beneath the hills, and became smaller with each generation. The country which is said never to have had a pogrom (not true, in fact: there was one in Limerick) because of this descendency from the thirteenth tribe, because of the great affinity between the Irish and the Jews, and the three great obsessions they have in common: sex, literature and a monopoly on God. There may be something in all that, but I have to say that if a tribe of Israel was lost I never missed it. Don't get me wrong. Me and the Jews go a long way back, and by and large they are a healthily sceptical lot who enjoy themselves with an abandon that is only possible if you know the world is against you. It's the religious ones with ringlets that I find hard to stomach. It was the Jews who first stumbled across me when I embarked on this career, and for a while things were fairly intense between us. But no marriage can last for eternity, and when I got some of my big breaks and a shot at world domination they were understandably miffed. I felt bad about it at the time, but I had no choice. I had a chance to push myself beyond the boundaries of possibility, to be more than a footnote in a theological encyclopaedia; I had a mission to justify my existence. That was a long time ago and most of them have got over it by now, apart from the ones with the ringlets who still go about with the bitter expression of the abandoned first wife of a novelist made good, pretending that they are the chosen ones and believing that a choice once made is forever. Who did the choosing? Not me. It was an accident, in the way of all love. The choice came later, in the way of all love. You cannot choose to love, but you can choose to abandon and, if you have any sense at all, you will. Like everything immortal, love is mutable.

I have wandered. There was a reason for bringing the Jews into this, but I've forgotten it for the moment. It wasn't anything very obvious, nothing to do with the camps or anything like that although I know that is what is expected of me, but I won't rise to it. You all supposed that if I existed I would have done something about the camps. Even the Rabbis put me on trial and declared me dead (earning my admiration in the process), but what was I supposed to do? The earth is not my domain. Death and suffering are not tragedies in my eyes. The camps were human: they were your responsibility, not mine. They were within the scope of your interference, not of mine. I may be capable of noticing every sparrow that falls from the sky, but I'm not necessarily in the business of giving each one a coronary by-pass, and I'm not overcome with sorrow at the sight of it. If I had to mourn every tragedy in the world there wouldn't be time for anything else. Who on earth, I'd like to know, started the rumour that God is compassionate? It is one of those lunatic ideas which grew with Christianity, because a lot of those attracted to early Christianity were people with more compassion than sense. Those asinine, self-centred martyrs. How do they think I felt? Have you ever watched someone being torn limb from limb and at the same time declaring that they are suffering for you? I thought I had made it clear that I wanted no blood sacrifice. How could I possibly afford the luxury of compassion? It was not my intention to raise this subject at all, and now that I have I should not have spoken of the camps in the past tense. These things are not in the past. I can see camps at this moment. Not on the same scale, but camps none the less. These things are part of your condition.

Blow all that. It isn't what I was thinking of. Yes. Thingy. What's his name? Dan Fieselbaum. That was the reason I mentioned the Jews in Ireland. Nice chap. Got in over his head a bit when he entered a partnership with Roxy Dixon. A good enough architect though, in a practical sort of way. He was the one who knew how to specify the cladding and browbeat the site managers. He was a good worrier, which was exactly the sort of foil that a character like Rory needed. The junior architects in the firm came to Dan with their problems, as they came to Rory with their ideas.

The offices of Dixon Associates were on Eden Quay, and from the outside they had the dilapidated appearance of the buildings on either side. There was a discount sweetshop on the ground floor called The Candy Bar, and buses stopped outside on their way to the hard suburbs of North Dublin. But that was only a façade, a complicated joke which made the interior even more of a shock to your system. Once you passed through the opaque, piss-stained door you were on another planet. Those offices were designed not just to impress but to make you feel gauche and ill-at-ease and, if you were a potential client, to make you feel that you knew nothing about architecture. Every gimmick was employed: white enamel flooring and glass and wire staircases and polished concrete walls and vases of strelitzia and ginger and a receptionist who looked like an extra from Barbarella, Ingo Maurer lighting and Rei Kawakubo furnishing. And if you were privileged, you passed through the atrium of awe and discomfort where assistants in Issey Miyake shirts bent over their drawing board, and you were shown into Rory's office, where you found huge sofas and inoffensive paintings and a reassuring mess across his comforting wooden desk. By this the visitors were manipulated from disappointment on the outside to bewilderment

148

on the inside to complaisance in the inner sanctum and, by the time Rory had shaken them by the hand and bathed them in his smile, they would have agreed to almost anything. It was a progression not dissimilar to the one I designed for heaven.

Now Dan was in charge and the office was in despondency and chaos. The strelitzias were dropping and the receptionist's lipstick no longer looked as though it had been applied with conviction. There were attempts to carry on with the projects in hand. Clients were faxed and telephoned to reassure them the practice was continuing as normal, but the truth was that no one was sure what would happen. Rory had kept a fifty-one per cent share in the firm which would be inherited by Helen, and no long-term decisions could be taken without her. In the week following Rory's death it had not been possible to approach her. Andy McGrath had called in at the office to say that she should be left alone until after the funeral. And at the funeral, just as Dan was about to speak to her, Corinna's body had been found.

Not all of the staff turned up on the following day and those who did were sent home again by Dan, apart from his personal assistant. He didn't think it was likely that any work could be achieved in the atmosphere of shock that pervaded the office that morning. The phone never stopped ringing, with clients and contractors who were worried by the newspaper reports, and journalists hungry for something to put in the next day's edition. Dan spent the day trying to deal with them, feeling hopelessly out of his depth. He kept wondering what Rory would have said, and how Rory would have coped. Rory would have laughed the whole thing off, would have asked anyone who was seriously worried to call in for a glass of champagne and told them stories, would have pretended that there was no crisis at all. Was he pretending, or had he really been someone for whom a crisis was of no importance? If so, how had he survived? Dan couldn't see how you could ignore danger and manage to survive.

In the afternoon he sent his assistant down to The Candy Bar for the evening paper. The story he was looking for was in the right hand column of the front page. The headline read, 'Doubts Over Corinna Dixon Suicide'. The story wasn't based on anything the police had said but on rumour and conjecture and gossip that the journalists had picked up in the bar of the Commodore, and from talking to Corinna's neighbours in Gavinstown. Dan thought it was odd that, if it had been so easy for the press to establish that Corinna could not have killed her father and if it was likely Corinna had not killed herself either, the police had made no statement. He thought it was odd, but his view of human nature wasn't perverse enough to guess that the police were waiting to see what came to the surface in the papers before they concocted their own version of events.

Dan pushed the paper away and went to the window. His shirt was sticking to his back in the afternoon heat and the light was bouncing off the Liffey. In the middle of the river six or seven boys were lounging on and diving off a raft made of hardboard and barrels. He began to worry that they might catch something from the filth of the river water or that they might drown, and wondered whether their mothers knew what they were up to. And then, while he was watching them laughing and cursing and pushing each other off the raft, whooping and blinding, he stopped worrying for five minutes. He didn't envy them their happiness: they were creatures with the pallor and muscle and ragged underpants of a childhood spent in a tower block. No doubt their day on the raft was no more than a day off from sniffing glue and joy-riding. He did, however, see something of Rory in them. It was in the way they

150

stretched their skin to the sun like a fox on a stone wall, oblivious to the abuse behind them and the hard life in front of them. It was in the way that their actions were undertaken for the sake of the moment, unconscious of the consequences, aware perhaps that no consequence is insuperable.

The raft drifted below the river wall out of his sight, and he turned away from the window in time to see Andy McGrath sway gingerly up the glass staircase.

'Grand day,' Andy said.

Dan smiled involuntarily, feeling the sun on the back of his neck through the glass. It was not a grand day but a terrible day, and no day for smiling, but you couldn't take the goodness from the heat of the sun.

'Is there a drink in the house?' Andy said, making straight for Rory's office, where he knew he would find one. He was sweating from the heat and from climbing the stairs, but more than that; if you were an animal you could have detected the taint of fear in his sweat. He emerged with a glass in his hand and said, 'It's as quiet as the grave in here. Where are all the young buckos?'

'They were a bit upset. I sent them home.'

'Best place for them, with the day that's in it.' It was not clear from his tone whether Andy was referring to the weather or the aftermath of Corinna's death.

'I'm glad you came,' Dan said. 'I've been trying to get you on the phone.'

'There's nothing like being wanted.' Andy hit his foot against a metal waste-paper basket, and in the clang of the basket as it fell over it became evident that he was drunk: it was the helpless way in which he watched the spillage, in the awkward sidestep he made. For a moment, as he steadied himself, he seemed unsure where he was or why he was there. The momentary loss of purpose alarmed and sobered him.

Dan called to his assistant who was at the other end

of the studio, sharpening pencils. 'Toby, you can go home now. There isn't anything else we can do today. I'll lock the place up.'

'Hold on a minute,' Andy said. 'Toby might be the man who can help me.'

Toby laid down his sharpener and pushed his spectacles up the bridge of his nose, trying to catch Dan's eye for some indication of how he should react, but Dan wore an expression that was blank with impatience. He had reasons for wanting to speak with Andy in private.

'Do you know,' Andy said, 'the small blue notebook Rory had? You wouldn't be able to lay your hands on it? There's a couple of numbers in it I want.'

Without any guidance from Dan, Toby automatically prevaricated. 'You'd have to ask Kanichi,' he said. 'He does all Rory's stuff.'

Then Dan released him with a gesture of permission. 'Have a look anyway,' he said. 'Try one of the drawers in the secessionist desk.'

For the ten minutes that Toby was hunting the notebook in Rory's office the other two men said nothing. Dan knew already what he had to say, and he tried to make use of the time to judge how he should say it. Andy stared at a drawing that had been left out on a board. When Toby had reappeared he said, 'Tell me one thing. I've always wondered. Why do all the men in architectural drawings wear flared trousers?'

'It's not us,' Toby said. 'It's Letraset.' He was holding the notebook in his hand, but Andy was making a show of attaching no importance to the fact.

'Is that so?' he said, and it was barely perceptible that his eyes slid in the direction of the notebook for an instant, checking that it was the one he wanted.

Dan felt pricks of heat on his face at the mention of the Letraset men. He wondered how long Rory would have to be dead before he would be able to think of him without these flushes of grief. The men in flared trousers had been the basis of one of Rory's jokes. He used to tell people that the firm employed an agoraphobic visualiser who had not left his house since the seventies.

'Is this the book you wanted?' Toby said.

'Oh, thanks,' Andy said, as if he had forgotten. He took the book carelessly and slid it into his pocket. 'I may as well take it with me,' he said. 'It won't be wanted here.' Dan seemed not to notice. He was bracing himself to broach the subject that was on his mind.

When they had heard the door down stairs bang shut behind Toby, Dan said, 'I wanted to ask you about your friends.'

'My friends?' Andy sounded puzzled, as if he couldn't pin down the meaning of the word.

'In the North. The shopping centre in Carrigraine.'

'Oh, that.'

'I can't seem to get hold of them. I've been trying for a week. Everyone else, all the other clients, have been phoning every day, but that lot won't even return my calls. I wondered if you had any idea what was going on.'

'Why should I?' Andy seemed sober all of a sudden. He was on the defensive, putting his glass down on the desk beside him as if he couldn't afford the marginal loss of competence that would come with another sip of the whiskey.

Dan hesitated. He had had a feeling that this wasn't going to be easy. He had had little to do with the project in Carrigraine. It was Rory who had flown north for all the meetings, but he knew that Andy was somehow involved, that the commission had come through Andy's contacts. Matters were still at an early stage: the footprint had only just been accepted by the planners and the contracts were about to be signed. It was crucial at this tender stage that the project went ahead.

With a potential fee of more than two million there was a chance that it might ensure the survival of the practice. If Dan could pull it off he might be able to get the finance to buy out Helen's share in the firm. Otherwise he would be just another unemployed architect traipsing the streets.

'Because,' he said, measuring and worrying each word before it hit the air, 'you are a director of the development company.'

'Am I?' Andy was almost mocking him. 'I lose track of these things.'

'Look,' Dan said.

Andy interrupted him with the same word. 'Look, I'll be straight with you. The whole thing is a dead duck. If I was you I'd drop it.'

Dan exploded. 'We can't. What about the contract? We need this thing, and we can do it, Rory or no Rory.'

'He didn't tell you, so?'

'Tell me what?'

'Rory was about to drop it himself.' Andy's eyes were sliding towards every part of the room except where Dan stood.

'Why?'

'Why schmy.'

Dan winced at what he rightly took to be an anti-Semitic dig.

Andy continued. 'For the sake of sweet Jesus, are you a child or what, asking why? You're out of your depth bucko. Did you not have a look at the tenders? Did you not notice anything?'

'I thought the ones we were accepting were a bit high.'

'A bit high? God spare us. It wasn't only the end of your dick they cut off, or maybe that's where your brains were in the first place? You didn't notice that the contractor had never built anything bigger than a cowshed before, that he had no experience of project management, that he wouldn't know an RSJ from a suppository?'

In another situation Dan would have thrown the man out for his insults, but there was more at stake here than racism and fine feelings, and in some senses it was better to hear out loud what he knew was said behind his back. He managed, just, to channel his anger into hauteur and said, 'So? We appoint another contractor.'

'You aren't getting the message here. Let me give you a few hints. The projected Meadowsweet Shopping Centre is to be built at Carrigraine, a Republican suburb of the notorious city of Belfast. The other contractors mysteriously withdrew their tenders. The planning application went through without a murmur of disapproval. The money to build it came out of nowhere in the middle of a recession. Am I getting through to you, or do you need me to spell out the acronym?'

'No.' Dan flushed red at his own naivety, with shock at the dawning of what should have been evident to him, in anger that was lost in frustration and impotence.

Andy was still talking at him. 'You're out of your depth bucko. Rory could have handled it maybe, but if you're the man in charge we'll all end up with a rod of semtex up our arses.' Andy leered for the killing blow. 'No great temptation for the married men amongst us.' He winked. 'I'll be off now,' he said. 'It wouldn't do for me to be found in here without a chaperone.'

Dan was beyond insult, racist or homophobic. The momentum of what had just been revealed to him was carrying his mind to other conclusions. He glanced at the newspaper nearest to him, which was open at a photograph of Rory. The smiling head, the unaffected smile, the dangerous eyebrows that met in the middle.

Andy was halfway down the glass stairs when Dan called, 'Wait. Wait a minute. If that's all true, isn't it obvious?'

'Isn't what obvious?'

'Maybe Rory couldn't handle it. They don't know who killed him yet, for certain. Maybe it had something to do with this. Do the police know about Carrigraine?'

'I'd stay out of it if I was you. If the boys had him on a list he wouldn't have died like that. It isn't their style. And they aren't the sort of people you want to start accusing of anything. You want to stick to what you know about. Do a nice drawing, there's a pet.'

Andy negotiated the rest of the stairs. He hadn't meant to be so venomous with the other man, but it had been necessary. He couldn't have let Dan see the corner he was in, and attack is the easiest form of defence. He couldn't say that he disliked Dan exactly. He had nothing personal against Jews or gayboys, and as gayboys went Dan was as inoffensive as you could hope for. There was nothing that you could call feminine or coy about him, but all the same you never knew where you were with a fella like that. He wouldn't have had anything to do with a fella of that persuasion if it hadn't been for Rory's sake. Whatever possessed Rory to take him on in the first place? There were plenty of normal architects around the place he could have employed.

Parallel to these thoughts, as Andy passed through the street door and out into the sunshine and as the pleasure of having insulted Dan faded from his bloodstream, the jitters began to creep up on him again and he wished he had finished off the remains of his drink. He stumbled into his car and told his driver to take him to Leinster House. The bar there would be quiet at this time and he could get smashed out of his head in peace.

The driver nodded and pulled out, cutting across the front of a green bus, while Andy sweated in the back, oblivious to the style of his driving. The afternoon traffic was still light and Leinster House only minutes away.

If Andy had been the sort of person who notices the expressions on the faces of his minions, he would have seen that his driver's aspect was somewhat brooding. Having to wait outside the offices of Dixon Associates had set him reminiscing about something. It had to do with Rory, but only slightly. Where Rory passed, his thumbprint was always left in the flesh of those whom he had encountered, sometimes so faintly that it was barely discernible, even by the one who was marked. A long time ago, Rory had had a ten minute conversation with this man while they were waiting for Andy outside a house in Rathgar, the result of which was that the driver's engagement had been broken off. Not that Rory had encouraged him to do so or even that the engagement had been mentioned in the conversation, but Rory had said something about having to see yourself clearly in any situation, and when you lost sight of yourself, that was the moment to cut your losses and run. Rory was thinking about a building he had been negotiating with the South Korean government, but he had said it with such feeling and in such a general way that the driver, troubled by his engagement, had applied it to his own case. Unknown to him, however, his affianced was pregnant at the time and, to save her pride, she took the boat for him and had an abortion. No one can speculate with any accuracy how happy that man would have been if he had married that girl and had that child, nor could anyone say that he wouldn't have come to the same decision without a chance conversation with Rory Dixon in Rathgar on a wet Wednesday. In isolation, the case for Rory having been the instrument of his fate is a weak one, but if you had been watching Rory as closely as I did you would see that that did tend to be the sort of effect he had on people. He was, by virtue of his energy, a natural catalyst, licking his way round sensibilities like a tongue of fire on a dim apostle. By and large it was unintentional, but he was aware of his own capabilities, and

157

he was capable of exploiting them when his interest was aroused.

Five Return from a Greek Holiday

Sunburnt and tired, the Delahunty family waded through the baggage hall of Dublin airport on their return from an eleven day bargain break on the island of Corfu. Mike Delahunty pushed the trolley and his sister Imelda walked slightly in front, carrying all the passports. Dolly, Mike's wife, held a little girl by the hand on either side of her. The children were almost identical in looks and height and were often mistaken for twins. They were in fact cousins, one being Imelda's daughter and the other Dolly's. It was when they spoke that their difference became evident. Dolly's child spoke like her mother, in the whingeing voice of the Barrow estuary. Imelda's child produced the whine of a Stockwell comprehensive school. The purpose of the holiday had, in part, been reconciliatory. Mike had lost contact with his sister for ten years, since the time when she went to England pregnant and unmarried. She had made good in the interim and now had a shop of her own in Brixton, selling spangly frocks and outsize shoes to nightclub queens when she wasn't vogueing on the stage of the Fridge on Saturday nights among the muscle clones. She had come home for the first time the previous Easter for her father's funeral, and that was when she and Mike had planned the holiday. Now

159

that old Delahunty was dead and Mike had the garage, there was no reason that they shouldn't resume their sibling relationship.

The holiday had been a success. Imelda knew how to have a good time and had dragged Mike and Dolly off to nightclubs and parties every evening of their stay. Mike was amazed that, although she professed never to have been to Corfu before, she seemed to know people everywhere they went. Or at least that people were always coming up to say hello to her and kiss the air at the side of her head. 'Who was that?' he would ask, as the gentleman in the No. 2 haircut retreated. 'I'm not sure,' she might reply. 'I must know him from somewhere. I think he's called Paul, or Ned maybe. Everyone looks the same when they're sunburnt.' Mike would shake his head in disbelief. How could she be so casual about the coincidence of meeting an acquaintance so far from home as this? He himself had been to Corfu four times now without meeting a soul he recognised, and if he did meet someone he was sure he'd be talking about the wonder of it for seven days afterwards.

Mike kept his eyes to the ground as they passed through the customs hall, even though there wasn't an official in sight. He hated this part of the journey. You heard terrible stories. What if someone had slipped something into one of the bags when he wasn't looking? What if they were watching him through a hidden camera and could see the worry and what must seem like guilt on his face? What if he had to be taken away and have a man in a rubber glove ferret around in his hole? At the thought of it, his sphincter contracted in a spasm of fear, and then he remembered that he still had a bit of the runs, and it would serve the bastards right if they went messing with that end of him. He was so engrossed in these thoughts, and in concentrating on rectal control, that they had passed through the

160

automatic doors without his noticing and out into the little corral that was surrounded with other people's waiting relatives.

He nodded at the luggage and said to Dolly, 'Mind that. I want to get a paper.'

The truth was that he wanted to go to the lavatory, but so as not to seem to be hurrying for it he went and bought the evening paper first and went through the door of the gents' as if it were an afterthought. Once inside he had to rush to get himself seated on the apparatus in time, hoping that there was no one in the other stalls to hear the noise he made. When the worst of it was over he unfolded the paper for a glance at the headlines. He wasn't expecting much, but it would be nice to know what had changed in the world in the time he'd been out of it.

The name Dixon jumped at him off the page. It was someone he knew, he was sure. Corinna? That must be the daughter of the fella who had the house at Innish. There it was: it said Innish. It must be the same people so. God, that was a fright, a young girl like that killed. He remembered now, he'd seen her father only the other day, the day they left for Corfu. Dolly'd wanted him to shut the garage, but he kept it open for the morning seeing as the plane wasn't going until six and all his packing was done the night before. Dixon came in very slowly in that car of his, the blue Spider, and said there was something wrong with the brakes. He had a look at them and they were cut through. He fixed them easily enough and put more fluid in, but he and Dixon shook their heads over it and wondered who could have done such a thing: vandals perhaps, or gurriers out from the town. He told Dixon to report it to the police, but Dixon didn't seem unduly bothered by it, and drove off in the direction of Hook Head.

Mike half-read the first paragraph, distracted by the memory of his encounter with Dixon and worried that

161

Imelda and Dolly would be getting impatient outside. He would get Dolly to read it to him properly in the car. He felt great excitement as he hitched his trousers up, to think he had a connection with a tragedy that was in the papers. That'd show Imelda that London wasn't the only place in the world to go for a bit of sensation. He washed hands that were unfamiliar to him. The ingrained dirt of the garage had only just faded after nearly a fortnight of being soaked in the sea and the backs of them were an even tan. Dolly was always saying she was ashamed to be out with him and his dirty hands. Well, she'd better make the most of it, because they'd be back to normal tomorrow. He took a last look at his jet-setter's fingernails and dashed back out to the women, waving the evening paper and nearly crashing into an American with enough luggage to ballast a lightship.

'Guess what?'

'What happened to you?' Dolly said. 'I thought you went to get the car.' The girls were trying to drag her towards the sweet counter. They had had to make do with Greek chocolate biscuits for the duration of the holiday and the sight of familiar confectionery was driving them wild. Dolly was irritated from having to restrain them, and Imelda was no help. She was sitting at a distance, absorbed in a critical study of her own legs, thinking that the tan didn't really go with her shoes and wondering whether it was worth getting another pair out of the baggage. 'For God's sake,' Dolly said. 'Go and buy the children a bar. They have the arms pulled off me and you went off with all the Irish money.'

'Look at the paper,' he said, feeling for change in his pocket at the same time in automatic response to his wife's command. 'That Dixon young wan is killed. The druggy wan from Innish.'

'No great loss.' Dolly was not in the mood for

sympathy. 'They want Curly Wurlys, and if there's none of them they want Duckula ice pops.'

By the time he had bought the sweets and found the car and arranged everyone inside it and been shocked by how much he was being charged for leaving it at the airport and had Dolly telling him that she'd told him so and he should have left it outside Karen Lee's house in Portmarnock and got a taxi, by that time he had forgotten about the evening paper. It wasn't until they were halfway down the road to Wexford that the subject came up again.

Dolly was sitting beside him doing most of the talking, turning to Imelda now and again so that she wouldn't feel left out of things in the back seat with the children. Imelda was half-listening, half-looking out at the countryside, remarking every now and again on some great change which had sprung up in the landscape since she had moved to London. It was in this disconnected idleness that she picked the paper up from where Mike had thrown it on the back window-shelf and began to read. 'Oh fuck me pink,' she said, not loudly, almost as if she had been unconscious that she said it.

'Imelda!' Dolly turned around to give the other woman a full view of her outraged expression. 'There's children present. Have a bit of consideration, please. Marcella isn't used to that kind of language.'

'I am so,' Marcella said, in an attempt to defend her aunt, but her mother wasn't listening. Neither was Imelda, who was staring into the paper, her lips moving in time as she sped through the paragraphs.

'Imelda!' Dolly said again. 'What is it?' Her question was motivated, not from enquiry, but from the need to draw her sister-in-law's attention. Dolly didn't like to be ignored.

'What?' Imelda said. 'Nothing. It's nothing. Just someone I knew is dead is all.'

163

Good Christ, Mike was thinking, is there anyone she doesn't know?

Dolly was straining to peer at the newspaper. She was surprised at the size of the headlines. Earlier, she had thought that Mike was only referring to something he had read in the death columns. Now that he had passed thirty, Mike was getting to the age when people read such things. She could see now that Corinna's death was a subject of importance and she could see why Mike had come rushing at her waving the paper in the air, but she wasn't going to admit it.

'Oh,' she said. 'That Dixon wan.' She sounded as though she knew already everything that was to be known.

Mike turned for a second to look at his sister, but Dolly told him to keep his eyes on the road. Mike said, 'How did you ever come across her?' He seemed a bit aggrieved. This should have been the scandal on which he had the inside story.

'I didn't,' Imelda said. 'I knew him.'

'Him?'

'Rory. It's nothing. Just I knew Rory, a long time ago.'

'Oh.' Mike was still at cross-purposes with her, still assuming that there had only been one death and that Imelda meant she had known Corinna by proxy. He remembered his intention to have Dolly read him the full article. 'Read it out,' he said. 'I didn't have a chance for a good look at it.'

Imelda couldn't imagine herself reading it out loud. It had been bad enough to read it to herself. She handed the paper to Dolly, who began by reading the headline and continued in a voice that was not her own, a more halting and careful voice in which the pronounciation of the words was mangled by her caution. Words that she would use every day became alien as they transposed themselves from the page to the open air. Not that she seemed to notice. She was pleased with her reading voice, since the meaning of her speech was clear to herself and she had no conception that what was clear to her might not be evident to others.

Imelda wasn't listening, was trying to keep herself upright in a cataract of remembrance. Sometimes, under certain circumstances, she would tell people the story of her life. It would be at six in the morning after staggering out of the Scala cinema or Kinky Gerlinky, maybe over bacon sandwiches at Frank's Café in Covent Garden, with overcoats on to conceal whatever outrageous get-up they had worn in the club, dazed with amyl nitrate and Japanese beer and seven hours of dancing. It had to be with someone you could trust, preferably someone you had never met before and would probably never see again. In the world she occupied it was better to be a mystery, a creature who had been born fully-grown and clad in a laced leather catsuit. But there were times when she needed to tell the story, not necessarily as it had happened in reality but in a way which made sense of what she had become.

The linchpin of this story would be Rory Dixon. Well, it would be Rory Dixon. He was the only person she had met before she went to London whom she had considered remarkable in any way. She said that he was the spur which had caused her transformation from virginal decorousness over the garage to vamp-empress of Cold Harbour Lane. Certainly he had taken her virginity and, although he was not the father of her daughter, it was to him she had turned in her pregnancy. He was the first person not to treat her condition as a tragedy. More than that, when she couldn't stand the hostility of her father anymore and decided to go to London, he had given her money and arranged a job for her. As a parting present he gave her a pair of shoes with five-inch metal spikes where the heels should be. They weren't the sort of shoes that could be worn with

165

any comfort and certainly not if you were pregnant, but he told her that they were something to look forward to after the baby was born. It was exactly the sort of present that she needed most, something which made her feel that the rest of her life wasn't earmarked for drudgery and devotion to motherhood. Sometimes impatience would get the better of her and, even though she was eight months gone, she would lace herself into the shoes for a few minutes, just to go to the shop next door for a pint of milk. And maybe it was agony, but she felt that the shoes transformed her, disguised her so that she was no longer one more of the legion of pregnant Irish girls sheltering in the anonymity of the crowds of London. In the shoes she was not identifiable as anything. People would turn to look at her and wonder. And then one day a man came up to her, shyly, but with a glint of recognition in his eye, and asked her where she had bought them. In her innocence she thought at first that he wanted a pair for his wife, until they had been talking for ten minutes and her back was in agony from standing on the pavement in the heels, and it suddenly dawned on her that he wanted the shoes for himself. She claimed that that was the moment when the scales fell from her eyes and she saw the world which she was later to inhabit, the parallel universe of false eyelashes and fishnet stockings which became her career. It was a place which was mostly the domain of men, but there was room for a certain kind of woman who was prepared to stretch and drag her femininity into the sphere of sexual doubt and androgyny, to learn the art of the demi-vierge. And somehow, within this society, she had found contentment and a liveable life for her and her child. That story, of course, was not the truth in the strictest sense, but it approached the truth more nearly than a strictly chronological listing of facts.

In London it was assumed that she had invented a

name as exotic-sounding as Imelda Delahunty, but she was at home now, where her name meant no more than that she was the daughter of old Delahunty; and it didn't matter what shoes she wore, she would still be identified first as the girl out of the garage in Knockjames. She had intended to see Rory Dixon if she could, even though she was aware of the danger that he wouldn't live up to her memories of him. She felt that she owed him something, even if it was only the laying of his ghost. Only now that he was dead his ghost was beyond exorcism.

Dolly read and Mike drove and the little girls began to drift away into sleep propped one against the other in the back seat. In the third paragraph it was revealed that Rory Dixon was dead also and Mike was taken aback by that, and would have made some appropriate exclamation if it weren't that Dolly was too immersed in the act of reading to be interrupted. When it was revealed in the fourth paragraph that the cause of his death, within hours of Mike having seen him, had been a severed brake cable, the car made a little, almost imperceptible swerve and Mike made use of the oath for which his sister had been reprimanded earlier. He, however, being more sensible of the prejudices of his wife, felt obliged to swear silently, and that was maybe why the invective coincided with an involuntary twitch on the steering wheel.

Dolly looked up to see what had caused the deviation. 'You're driving too fast,' she said. 'You'll have us all in the ditch.' She satisfied her accusation by looking at the speedometer. Fifty-eight miles an hour, which was three over the legal limit.

'Sorry,' he said, letting the car decelerate.

'Is something the matter?' she said, seeing the consternation on his face.

'Trouble,' he said.

'With the car?'

'No. The car is grand. Don't you remember? I told you about it the day we left. That fella in the paper. The dead fella. I fixed his brakes for him the day he died. It was the day he died, the day we left, wasn't it?'

She looked at the paper to check the date. It was the same. She couldn't remember now if he had told her about fixing the brakes. He was always telling her what cars he fixed and she never listened.

'Why is it trouble?' she said.

'I don't know. Maybe I didn't fix them right and it's my fault. In any case, it doesn't look too good for the garage if I'm blamed for it.'

She said the first words that her instinct put into her mouth. 'There's no reason anyone should know it was you.'

'They'll find out. They'll be going round the garages asking questions. They might have been already only we weren't there. I'm surprised they weren't waiting for me at the airport.'

'Don't be dramatising yourself,' she said. 'If they come and ask you, you can tell them. You've nothing to hide. And if they don't come no one need be any the wiser. You can always say you forgot.'

'Forgot what?' Imelda said. She had been so quiet in the back that they had assumed she was asleep with the children. They had been speaking too softly for their words to be heard by Imelda above the sound of the engine, but she had come out of her reverie and leaned forward in time to hear the last sentence.

'Nothing at all,' Dolly said with an unreal airiness. 'We were only talking about the garage.' Then she began to remark on the events described in the paper, showing signs of nothing more than the normal interest of a distant neighbour of the dead.

Mike drove on in deep discomfort. He wasn't satisfied by his wife's instruction not to go to the authorities with what information he had. She would say that it

168

was none of their business but maybe it was, and maybe things would be worse in the long run if he didn't make a clean breast of it. And on top of everything else he badly wanted to go to the lavatory again. He would have liked to drive faster, to end this terrible car journey as quickly as possible and see what was waiting for them at the other end, and be able to sit in the comfort of his own bathroom, contemplating the row of crocheted toilet roll covers and the framed transcription of Kipling's 'If' on the back of the door. In his present state he couldn't think, and what he needed was the sort of familiarity which made thinking unnecessary.

Power

David Kennedy was reeling. Thoughts jumped in and out of his mind with no coherence or sequence. He had spent the morning at the barracks in Gavinston not so much answering questions as making utterances in response to questions. That he had not murdered his wife was easy to establish. He had been seen leaving Innish, and his brother vouched that he had returned the car to him about forty minutes later. His brother then drove David and the baby back to the council estate, and stayed with him for an hour or more. This was confirmed by the woman who lived across the road. She had spent the afternoon waiting for her daughter to arrive from Dublin, and had looked out of the window every time she heard a car engine.

The man who questioned him was sympathetic, even tactful. He kept saying that he knew how hard it must be and what a strain David must be under, but if he could remember anything, anything at all no matter how trivial, it might be of some help. At the beginning there was still a small possibility that Corinna had killed Rory, and so he was asked if he knew why his wife would want to murder her father. He wanted to tell them what he knew of the abuse, of the way in which Rory had distorted her mind. But what he knew was mostly supposition, arrived at from what he had heard her say when she talked in her sleep, combined with her attitude to her father and to sex, and the odd hint that she had dropped when she was trying to be hurtful to him. And it wasn't only the paucity of his knowledge that prevented him from talking. There was Corinna to consider. She wouldn't have wanted those things to be known. He didn't see why he had to betray her now, just because she was dead.

And in consideration of Corinna he couldn't tell them anything which compounded their idea of her guilt. He thought that she couldn't have cut the brakes, because he knew nothing about the repair or the second cut. The police had been selective in the evidence they had released. Corinna had wanted to kill her father, had wished him dead often, but as far as David was concerned she couldn't have done it, so what was the point of saying that she would have?

He stammered and apologised and looked about him distractedly at the posters for rabies, and foot-and-mouth, and safe driving. Other officers came and went, speaking to the one who was interviewing him for a moment, in whispers, by the door. The line of questioning changed after each interruption. By degrees it became clear that the patricide theory wasn't going to stick, and then that the case for Corinna's suicide was falling apart. It seemed that the more answers the investigators found the less they knew. Then David was asked, as a matter of course, where he had been on the morning of Rory's death and he answered that he had been at work. He wasn't being evasive, only disconnected, but he caused suspicion when it transpired that work took him to Innish and he could have had access to the car, and things were made worse when his interrogator was told at the next interruption that he had been trained as a mechanic.

He wasn't in a state to lie, nor had he the courage to tell the truth. He was afraid to speak at all because he felt he had no control over what he might say. He

172

knew he would have to decide one way or another, and that his decision would affect the rest of his life. He thought it odd that the moment to decide should come now, and that the decision should be whether to own up or not. The act of cutting the brakes seemed to have involved no decision at the time. It had seemed inevitable. He had done it for Corinna. He had wanted to free her of her past so that they could be happy together, and for a long time before he had been fanta-sising about ways to kill Rory, and that morning it had seemed like fate that the blue Spider had been parked out of sight of the house. I heard him pray as he cut through the cable: he prayed that it might work, that it might kill him, and that Corinna might forget him once he was dead. He offered it up and left it in my hands.

The man across the table was waiting for his answers, one hand holding a pen, the other hand flat on the table. Then the fingers of the flat hand retracted, like the hand of a baby clutching at blankets. David thought of Sid, and then he knew that he couldn't let himself be accused of the murder; if he went to prison the child would have no one. And the thought of Sid and the thought that his family had been destroyed brought tears to his eyes, and he heard himself sobbing. He looked at the face of the man who was interviewing him and saw that it was a face full of compassion.

And David said, 'I can't do this. I can't do this now. I can't think. If you give me some time I'll tell you whatever you want. But I want to go home now. I'm sorry.'

And the other was inclined to believe him. He felt bad about the interrogation, about questioning a man who had been through so much so recently. And he hadn't liked making accusations at this man. It was plain that David Kennedy couldn't harm a fly, that the object of this exercise was to fill reams of paper with

173

questions and answers, to cover all the possibilities so that no one could accuse them of carelessness afterwards. It was wrong to torture this man for the sake of bureaucracy. He decided to let him go.

They drove him back to his mother's house where he had left Sid. The front door was open as it had always been in his mother's house, and he only had to push it to let himself in. His mother was down in the sitting room with Sid on her knee, the two of them laughing at some game she was playing, too engrossed in each other to notice him standing in the doorway. That was when the decision came to him. He would confess. Sid's life would be far better off without him. The whole thing was his own fault. If he hadn't cut the cable that day Corinna would still be alive. He failed to understand why Corinna had died. It would have made some sense if it had been suicide, because he had always known that she wanted to die. However, being used to blaming himself, he didn't need to understand why in order to think that he was in some way responsible. What right had he to bring up Sid when he had as good as caused the mother's death?

And she had known. He was sure that she had known what he had done. She had known that he had done it for her, and she should have been grateful. How was he to have guessed that she loved her father as much as she hated him, if she hated him at all, if it wasn't herself she hated? Looking at his mother and his child, David knew one thing: that he was in some way incompetent to deal with those whom he loved, that if he loved anything it would perish at his touch. He was afraid for Sid's survival, and thought that the child would be better off if his father was safely in prison.

And his mother. Had she not been right? Had she not told him that his marriage to Corinna would be a disaster? And in her goodness, once they were wed, had she not suffered to have them in an already overcrowded house, and been kind to Corinna for his sake? David couldn't think of anyone whose life had been made easier for knowing him, and couldn't see that he had earned a place in society. He wondered whether to leave the room quietly, before they saw him there, and return to the barracks to turn himself in.

His mother looked up, and said, 'It's yourself.'

'I have to go out again, Ma,' he said. 'Are you all right with the babby for a while?'

'He's no trouble.' Then she held Sid up and spoke close into his face, smiling and saying, 'You're not, so you're not. No trouble at all.'

'Right so,' he said, and turned to leave.

'David, wait. Will you not have a bite before you go? There'll be dinner in a minute if you wait. Do you have to be anywhere urgent?'

'I did it, Ma. I did it and I have to go and tell them.'

Hearing him, terror gripped her in the chest. She knew what he was saying to be impossible, but it gave her a fright to hear him say it.

'What?' she said. 'What are you saying? What did you do? You can't have done anything. You weren't anywhere near her.'

'Not that, Ma. But I was the cause of that anyway. I killed her father, and if I hadn't done it she'd still be alive.'

She stood up. 'Take the child,' she said, handing Sid to him and walking past him into the kitchen.

'Ma, what are you doing?'

'I'm making the dinner. You're not going anywhere without your dinner.'

'Ma, have sense.'

She turned to him with tears in her eyes. 'You don't have to. Nobody knows. I won't tell on you. No more need be said about it. It's nearly a fortnight now, and if they haven't found you out by now, there's a chance they never will.'

175

'Ma, they already know I used to be a mechanic. They've only just looked under the bonnet of the Spider. They'll find things. You know what it's like. A hair falls out of your nose or something and then they have you. I don't want all that. I'd be better off going in now and saving us all the worry.'

'You'll have your dinner first,' she said. 'You can't decide something like that on an empty stomach.'

He handed Sid back into her arms and kissed her wet cheek. They were not a demonstrative family, and he had not kissed his mother since early childhood, so the kiss was an act of significance. 'I'll see ye, Ma,' he said, and left the house.

He noticed everything as he walked back through the town: the windows of the houses above the shopfronts, the moss curling over the gutters, the shapes of the doorknockers in Priory Street – all the details but none of the people. He must have passed people and some he knew, but he saw none of them, only architectural details. As he climbed the hill to the barracks he found himself stepping between the cracks in the pavement. Step on a crack and break your mother's back.

The barrack orderly was the same man who had seen him leave not half an hour since. He asked to see the man who had questioned him earlier, and was told that he would have to wait. Detective Flynn had gone to his lunch and wouldn't be back for an hour. Was there anyone else he'd like to see? David said no, he would wait, and he sat on a hard bench with his back to the wall. While he waited his mind was blank. Thoughts came, but they were aborted before they could be formed; they dispersed into fragments beyond his grasp. In his mind's eye he watched these dissolving fragments of thought, thinking nothing.

He couldn't have said whether the hour he waited

seemed like a long time or a short time. When Detective Flynn spoke to him it was as though he had woken from unconsciousness.

'Mr Kennedy. What can I do for you?'

It took seconds for him to recall why he was there, looking up at the reassurance of the other man, and then he said, 'I remembered something.'

'Would you like us to go somewhere quiet? I'll see if there's a room.'

David nodded. He would like, above all, to go somewhere quiet.

When they were sitting again at the same table, with cups of sweet coffee before them, Flynn said, 'It's very good of you to come back to us like this. If we had half that sort of co-operation from all our witnesses there'd be no crime in the country at all.'

'I did it. I came in to tell you I did it. So you needn't be investigating anymore.'

'Did what Mr Kennedy?'

'All of it.'

It was natural to think that the poor man had lost his senses, that the death of his wife had driven him out of his mind. There was no way he could have done all of it. Flynn felt sorry for him and spoke gently.

'All what, Mr Kennedy?'

'It's my fault she's dead. But I only did it for her to begin with. I cut the brakes. If I hadn't, she'd be alive.'

Flynn drank from his coffee to mask his confusion. He had faith in his own judgement of character, and he had long judged David innocent. There was no way that this man could mean what he was saying. David looked lost altogether. What was he trying to do? Make sense perhaps of senseless acts by exaggerating his own culpability. Flynn was not expecting a reliable confession, but there was a possibility that some useful information might emerge.

'Maybe, Mr Kennedy, if you could start at the begin-

177

ning. I won't be taking a statement just yet, so take your time.'

David thought about it, and he was confused by the idea of the beginning. It was hard to say what the beginning had been. Did it mean the day he saw Corinna under the horse chestnuts and fell in love with her? Did it mean the first time it had occurred to him that the world would be a better place without Rory Dixon in it? David couldn't put those beginnings into words. He wasn't sure that he had any more to say than what had been said already. He had said that he had done it. What more could they want? Was he obliged to prove his own guilt?

'I don't know,' he said. 'What do you want me to say?'

'Maybe why you did it?'

'That's between me and her. I did it for her.'

'All right. How did you do it then?'

'It wasn't hard. It was so simple it was shockin'. I was delivering the letters and his car was round the side of the house, below the garden wall. I opened the bonnet and I cut the brakes.'

'With what? What did you use?'

'Cutters.' David said the word as if he was amazed that the question should need to be asked.

'And where did you get them?'

'I always have a few tools in the van. If anything goes wrong it's quicker to fix it yourself than wait for anyone to come out to you.'

'And then what did you do?'

'I went on with the round.'

'You didn't do anything else?'

'Like what?'

'How many cuts did you make?'

David looked at him as if the policeman had lost his marbles. Such a question made no sense. Why would he have made more than one cut? Perhaps there was a trick in it somewhere. David could think of no answer but the truthful one, but he spoke with a caution which undermined the veracity of his words.

'Just the one.'

'Did you notice anything about the cable? Was it in good condition?'

'I'd say so. It was a fairly new one. He kept that car up. You have to with cars like that. They break down every five minutes. Plenty of money. No bother to him.'

'You are sure you only made one cut in the cable?'

David nodded. He had thought that by now he would be in handcuffs in the back of a Black Maria. He had thought that Flynn would be glad of the enlightenment, but Flynn was looking more perplexed than he had all day.

Flynn stood up. He said, 'I have to make a couple of calls. Will you be all right in here? Do you want more coffee or anything?'

And then he was gone. He seemed to be away a long time. Maybe they were having trouble finding the handcuffs. David thought about the handcuffs that had come with his cowboy suit one Christmas when he was little. He wondered what had happened to the suit. His mother would know. He could ask her on one of the prison visiting days, and maybe she could still find it and Sid could have it when he was older. It was a good cowboy suit, with a real holster and everything, and a black waistcoat with fringes on.

Flynn was standing in the doorway, leaning on the handle as if he was waiting for David to come out of his daydream.

'There's just the one thing, Mr Kennedy. What day was it you cut the brakes?'

'The same day.'

'The day he died?'

'Of course the day he died. What other day would it be?'

'That's all right, Mr Kennedy. You can go home now. We'll send for you if we want you again.'

So David Kennedy went home, not to his own house but back to his mother, who fed him. He submitted to her care as he had submitted to Flynn's rejection of his confession, as he had submitted to his love for Corinna. He had no choice. The one time in his life he had exercised his power to change events had ended in disaster. I know the feeling. However, unlike me, he was wise enough to renounce his power after the first failure.

I am tired of this. I was never a being who succumbed to the thrill of a thriller, who suspended disbelief and engaged myself in the suspense of a fabricated mystery. Those other documents were easier: I am the Lord your God and I command you to obey this, that or the other arbitrary command. What has happened that I am come to this? And what next? God the game-show host?

I am tired of this, but I am sick of other things: of the illusion of power and glory; of being blamed for everything while being loved unconditionally; of people telling each other that God moves in mysterious ways. There is no mystery, only me, getting it wrong sometimes and right at others. And this, the account of one of my failures, is a confession as much as anything. And, like David Kennedy, I expect to be disbelieved, to be sent back to my mother and my son, to the place you choose to believe I occupy because your idea of me is the idea you are most comfortable with. After all, if there is no hope for me, what hope is there for you?

The Word Made Flesh and the Dissipation of Lust in the Aftermath of a Consummation

It had to be, in a text of this kind, that Jesus Christ would come into it sooner or later. The key to any understanding of the effect of Christianity on the world is that Christ was my only son. Being God, I could have as many sons as I like, or daughters for that matter. That I never repeated the experiment, and probably never will, is an indication of how disastrous the failure was. He is a nice boy, I admit, and he did his best, but we cannot predetermine the qualities which we would like our children to have and Jesus, for all his goodness, showed some catastrophic faults during his time on earth. In the first instance he was not a very good judge of character. I don't know how he managed to accumulate such a band of yapping nonentities around him. You would think by the law of averages that one of the apostles would have shown a bit of spark, but no; the Church was to be built on the teachings of a bunch of lily-livered half-wits. I can see that it isn't easy to attract disciples of the right kind. Anyone who is foolish enough to drop everything and go trotting after a bearded stranger is a fool indeed. But couldn't he have tried a bit harder in his recruitment? The fact was that his motives for choosing these people were constrained by another fault in his character. I am referring to his lack of sex drive, which was the last thing I had foreseen. That any son of mine should not be interested in sex defies the imagination, but it happened, and we have all had to live with the consequences.

I know there is speculation about his relationship with Mary Magdalene, and rightly so, but the fact is that she was a bit of a fag hag and he was amused by her conversation, and that was about all there was to it. If he had any erotic impulses at all they were in quite another direction, but so slight and so latent that they never came to anything. There was the occasional bit of drunken snogging with the Apostle John. Apart from that he kept himself to himself. Disliking sex, however, did not prevent him from using sexual motivation in the choosing of his followers. It is remarkable, if you lined them all up, how similar they were in looks and stature. Not that he realised what he was doing. He thought that, whenever he saw a fisherman standing about on the beach and the hairs rose on the back of his neck, it was divine guidance. The result was that his ministry was left in the hands of a pack of gooey-eyed sheep. The damage might have been averted, the cult could have disappeared without trace and left me in a position to try again, if it weren't for Paul.

If there were a hell there should be a place in it specially reserved for that man, Saul or Paul or whatever he likes to call himself. Nobody asked him to put his oar in. He was insane to start with, and then he fell off his horse and started hearing the voice of God. A lesser man would have found himself in a padded cell, but he managed to make a career of it. I concede that the marketing strategies were brilliant, but I do wish that he had discovered pyramid selling instead of religion. The world might be a better place by now.

Don't you see the confusion which I, indirectly, have

caused? You were created an animal in my image, out of my vanity and my loneliness. The years of my expectation, of your evolution, were happy years, years of looking forward to a function, to parenthood on a grand scale. And as an animal in my image you charmed me: moving, naked and elegant, across the earth, slaughtering to eat, fucking to reproduce, playing to amuse yourselves. If only that had been enough. But I was greedy in my ambition. I wanted you to know your God while you were still walking on earth. I had no business wanting such a thing, but it became a fixation. I wasn't satisfied that you would come to know me after your deaths. I had to interfere with the living. I knew that it wasn't going to be easy. There were no precedents for communication between the dimensions, so it was plain that there would be a certain amount of hit-and-miss, but I never envisaged the mess which has come about. All I have done is create a yearning in some of you to know me. I know now that such knowledge is impossible while you live. That is why the salvation of the world, or the only possibility of it, is in atheism.

And this confusion is compounded by the cult of Christ, and of Krishna and Buddha and other holy men. Because these beings have been so good, or because their mythologies have portrayed them as being so good, you are exhorted to be more Christ-like or Buddha-like or whatever. Why, if you are already made in the image of God, should you strive to be more like my son? The implication is that my son is an improvement on me. That is possible, but I can tell you from an intimate knowledge of him that he isn't. He depends too much on goodness, and he believes too much in me. He is an heir who will never inherit, and so he is weak, and so he fills his days with idealistic dreaming, growing older without the dignity of authority.

And you on earth, no longer seeing yourselves as

animals, are left with ideals you can never attain, feeling obliged to pay lip service to the concepts of justice, of democracy, of mortality, of ecology, of what you call humanity. Is there anything in nature which justifies vegetarianism? It is only a false sense of your own sanctity which propagates such philosophies. And by the pursuit of that sanctity you lose your dignity. And by what you call immorality, in a society which proclaims that sanctity, you lose your self-respect. It is rare that a being will escape these traps. Rory Dixon, by accident of upbringing and by character, did. His friend Andy McGrath became the worst that is possible: a man raised to have a conscience, who cauterized that conscience in the interest of material gain, and was left suspended in a state of semi-existence, believing in nothing and thinking subconsciously all the while that he was destined for hell. How could I build hell for the likes of him when the blame is my own?

He is not beautiful by any standard in the biological universe. There are creatures as fat who have a certain majesty and creatures as sluggish who have a certain grace and creatures as ugly of whom it can be thought that their ugliness is functional, but Andy McGrath is repulsive in a way that is unique to humans. Even if he were to slough his ridiculous politician's clothing there would be no improvement. If anything he looks worse naked, with his rolls of fat and gingery sparse body hair and blotched skin, and pustules, and genitals that seem to have been recently peeled, not to mention his ruched arse and yellow toenails. I look at him, and the many like him in Normandy, in Germany and America, and I feel that the whole of creation has been undermined. That is not my image, was not my intention. He is both a living insult to nature and a breathing reminder of my mistakes.

That is not all. Outward repugnance will often mask a perfectly acceptable mind, but in Andy McGrath's case his mind and body are in harmony. His thoughts, like his appearance, are a parody of my image: close enough to be recognisable and different enough to be hideous to me. His thoughts sear into my consciousness, mocking me for what I have lost.

The heart is flesh and I have no flesh, but even with such a handicap I can grieve for my mistakes. McGrath, all flesh, would seem to be without remorse. It is true that the vision of Corinna in her bath of blood appears in his mind from time to time, but he muses on this vision with complacency. It is part of the library of interesting spectacles in the collection of his reminiscences. It is true that he was hot with worry the day he went to see Dan Fieselbaum, but it was not his conscience which was worrying him. The existence of the blue notebook in hands other than his own was a threat to his freedom.

The notebook secure in his pocket, where his fingers slid from time to time to touch it for reassurance, he settled himself in the comfort and security of the bar in Leinster House. He wished that Rory were there. They could be laughing about the events of the past few days. Would Rory laugh over the death of Corinna? Well, perhaps not that, but other than that he would have loved his own funeral, and the funeral would have been a hundred times better had he been there. Were he here, Andy thought, but not as wistfully as you might think considering that Rory was supposed to have been his best friend. He took a slug at his whiskey and leaned back, and thought – but this is nice enough. This is the place to be. Sanctuary. Is there a law of sanctuary which applies to this place? Surely there is. Could they arrest me here, or would I have to come out of my own volition? I could stay here for years if I had to. Not that it's going to come to that. If I lose my seat the majority is lost and the government will fall. Immunity by proportional representation. Or could I keep my seat from a prison cell? They'd have to let me out to vote, I suppose. Don't be thinking about that. I never got caught before. There's no reason I should be caught now. There's a thing. If you go back. If you look for reasons. You can fuck as many women as you like. Fuck them till you're blue in the face. Maybe you're always looking for something else. She was the only one who fitted. It's odd that. That she fitted. I slid into her and we locked into place. A matter of my oul' fella having the same bend on it as her cunt. Me convex where she was concave. Would she still be the same, after all the time and having the child and all? Rory was the man. He knew a good thing when he saw it, and he stuck to it. But I was there first. And she can't have locked into him the way she locked into me. He was a different build altogether. I should know. I seen him at it often enough. But I was always only the warm-up man. He was the one they screamed and gripped the sheets for, while I lay to one side, limp, wasted and watching. Except for that one from Sligo who wanted the two of us at once. Not that it worked the way it does in the films. Too many legs in the way. Some things are better thought about than done. I was nearly smothered, and too near the boil to last. And too worried that things might get perverted. Give Rory his due, we had some close calls but we never did anything perverted. Though it was an effort at times to remember that it was the woman was supposed to be turning you on. God save us from women. I don't know if I would have suffered her the way Rory did. Not even for the sake of locking together like that. Though I suppose it was the closest I got to falling in love. Jesus thank fuck I was spared that anyway. But still, if you take things back, that must have been the start of it. That's all a barrel of shite anyway. There's too much psychoanalysis in the world as it is, much good it does anyone. I'm not sorry I did it, whatever the reason. I

186

did it, and that's that. I suppose it was shitting a bit near my own doorstep, but if I'm not caught, and I won't be, there's no more to be said about it. I'm not worried, just not drunk enough yet. Jesus the key. It's still in the other pocket. I suppose I should get rid of it. I should have shoved it back under the door, and they would have thought it fell out of the lock. I wasn't thinking. Wasn't thinking enough. There was a lot of things I should have done. I should have cut her in the wrists and not the throat. That would have made the suicide a certainty. But what could I do? How could I have kept her quiet all the time she was bleeding? I could have dropped the key on the floor when we all went back in the bathroom. A lesson learnt, I suppose. Still, it's all in hand. I wouldn't be the only one to swing if the truth came out. Fuck me, what's the world coming to if you have to worry like this every time you kill a girl? She's no loss. She said as much herself. And what difference? She was going to kill herself anyway. Why waste a death on suicide when someone else can have the pleasure of it? Things should go smoothly enough if the right people keep their traps shut. I wouldn't trust that little shit Fieselbaum as far as I could throw him, but I have him frightened out of his frilly knickers now, and that's the way to have them. How was I to know she was lying? If someone says they murdered their father, you'd expect to believe them. She obviously wasn't the full shilling. Like her mother. Am I imagining it, or did we really lock together like that? I wouldn't mind finding out. Now that Rory's out of the way, I suppose she'll be needing a bit of relief from somewhere. Women have no control if they don't get a regular fix. She pretends she doesn't like me, but that's a real sign a woman can't wait to get her hands on you. And it's all her fault. I only followed the girl into the bathroom to see if she was as good a fuck as her mother. What harm? The story is she had half the population of Gavinstown anyway. Just as well I didn't knock her up before I killed her. The forensic boys would have had a field day. Science would frighten you. I hope none of the stuff got stuck in the U-bend. They'll never take the sink apart. And if they do I can say that I nipped up for a wank earlier in the afternoon. That's a fright, if you think about it, all the men wanking in sinks all over the world. You'd never wash your face again if you had to think about all the people who'd pissed and wanked in your sink. What was his name? That fella who said he did it in every house he went to. Marking the territory, he said. Fucking intellectual. Heggerty or Fleggerty or something ending in gerty anyway. Fair play to him. There's not many would admit it. Admit nothing. The policy stood me in good stead. There's no reason to change now. It was worth it all the same. An experience, I suppose. Rory said you should experience everything if you could. I never killed a girl I knew before. I suppose the soot has gone out of killing strangers. There's a test of open-mindedness. You don't mind, old chap, if I slit your daughter's throat for the sake of experience? I don't know if it's a pleasure, but what is? It's done now. I should have left the fucking key behind. The man who never made mistakes never made anything. It's only a question of sitting tight for a while. The secret of success is sitting tight. Sooner or later the whole lot will come to you. And if you're sitting tight enough the bad can wash over you while you're putting the good in your pocket. Wouldn't it be a laugh if I put the key somewhere strange? The in-tray of the Department of Justice, just to see. No, the lads are doing a good enough job as it is. No point in complicating things for them. The river's the place for it. I should have planted it on Fieselbaum. There's a good precedent for blaming the Jews. No point in deviating from an old formula if it works. That's what gets me about the likes of Fieselbaum. It's greed, gluttony pure and simple. Why wouldn't they be happy shaggin' women like the rest of us? We could all go round shoving things up our arses and then where would the world be? Up shit creek, that's where. There's such a thing as natural law. Whatever else I did I never broke a natural law. The other law is made and unmade. I should know, being one of the men that make it. I could bring in a bill to repeal the murder law. That'd put us on the map. The country where you can kill who you like. The expense we'd save. Honesty. That's all it'd be. And no malingerers or gayboys or snivelling shites or nagging women. Of course, you'd have to kill all the right people at the beginning. You could have a purge just before the law came in so all the buckos who are out to get you are dead by the time it's on the statutes. There'd be no problem with reunification after that. The unionists would be begging to be let into the country. Bloodthirsty cunts the lot of them. I could sleep now. But if I don't get a feed in me first I'll have some head on me in the morning. Jesus Christ, what does that fella want?

'Excuse me. Mr McGrath?'

'What's the matter with you?'

'Telephone, Mr McGrath.'

'I'm not here.'

'It's a Mr Foley. He says it's urgent.'

'Does he? The fat bastard. All right, I'm coming. Give us a hand up.'

The minion held his hand out and by holding on to it Andy McGrath hauled himself to his feet, letting go a sour whiskey belch in the rising, and swayed in the direction of the telephone that was indicated to him.

Foley didn't sound well in himself. He wouldn't say much and his voice was staccato, the pitch of it uncontrolled. He insisted that Andy should meet him in half

189

an hour. He said that his car was parked on the north side of Parnell Square and that he would be waiting inside it. Then he hung up with an abruptness which confirmed the fear that had been evident in his voice.

It may have been the panic in Foley's voice which helped Andy McGrath to keep his mind under control. He had been bridling anxiety for twenty-four hours and it would have been easy for him to let himself go, but panic is not always infectious. There are times when the panic of another can make you cold and clear-headed with irritation. He was tempted not to meet Foley, thinking that whatever crisis had emerged would probably involve Foley alone and not affect himself. Foley would only have come to Dublin if his own neck was at stake. He was not the sort of man to put himself out to warn another of danger unless his own interests could be served. Then it occurred to Andy that it might be a fear of finding out the worst which was dissuading him from going to Parnell Square, and if that was the case it would be more sensible to go. Fear itself could well transpire to be his worst enemy.

He went by taxi as a precaution, as far as the top end of O'Connell Street, where he went into a shop and bought a bar of chocolate to give the taxi time to move on. He thought that Foley had been mad to suggest meeting in such a public place. It was more than likely that he would be recognised since his face was somewhere in the media just about every other day. The girl behind the counter in the sweetshop looked at him for a moment too long, knowing that he was some-one familiar but unable to remember who he was exactly. He was used to these double-takes in the street, and used to people deliberately not looking in his direc-tion because they did recognise him and it was the fashion in Dublin to ignore the famous. He would have to brazen it out, walk along the street as if he were early for an appointment and react with mock surprise when he saw Foley sitting in the car.

There were no pedestrians about on the north side of the square, and Foley had had the sense to park facing away from the pavement so that they couldn't be studied by any strollers who passed. Andy got into the passenger seat and offered the sergeant a piece of chocolate.

'Grand day,' he said. Until he had reason to do otherwise it was his intention to behave with a facetious calmness.

There were no pleasantries in Foley. The message he had come with burst out of him in his first utterance. 'The Dixon investigation has to be stopped.'

'Is that right?' Andy said, his voice wet with melted chocolate. 'Who says so?'

The sergeant was shaking. 'I'm being serious,' he said.

'Take hold of yourself, man. You know as well as I do that the thing is fixed. The investigation in hand at the moment will ask less questions than no investigation at all. You know yourself. What's up with you?'

'It has to be stopped. There's no two ways about it. It was you killed the girl. I know that.'

While Andy's mind was still racing for the most convincing rebuttal Foley said, 'Lookit,' and reached across to open the glove compartment. He took out a watch. 'You left that on the sink. I suppose it was when you were washing the blood off your hands.'

'What makes you think it's my watch?'

'Well,' Foley said. 'It'll be no harm to you if I give it in for fingerprinting so. And they could find out what the stain is on the back of it while they're at it.'

McGrath shrugged with what was meant to be carelessness, but when Foley held out the watch to him he took it and put it on his wrist.

'What did you do a thing like that for?' Foley said. 'I had the whole thing under control. Are you mad or what?'

'It's still under control.' McGrath sounded petulant. 'The file will be filled and the DPP is squared. There won't be any prosecution.'

'It has to be stopped.'

McGrath felt sick. He could taste the chocolate and the whiskey in the back of his throat and feel the bile in his stomach. His mind lurched from the first half of one sentence to the second half of another. He should explain himself. But explain what? There was no explanation that was fit to be aired. And what business was it of Foley's? The man had no right knowing anything. What had passed between him and Corinna was a private matter. That was the whole point. There was something in killing about bringing another person to the limits of their existence in the safe knowledge that they could never tell on you, or look you in the eye the next day. He had done it in the certainty that he would never be found out, that he would never have to rationalise it.

In his confusion he almost failed to see that there was no obvious connection between Foley knowing what he had done and Foley wanting the investigation stopped. If this was all there was to it, why had Foley come to him, white and shaking?

He said, more calmly than he had expected he would be able to, 'So what's all this in aid of? If you're trying to threaten me you haven't a leg to stand on. If I was up for murder anyway, it'd be no skin off my nose to tell them about your little coke deals and one or two other misdemeanours. It's sink or swim together. You know that.'

'I know that. It isn't me making the threats.'

'Who?'

'The boys. I had a visit from the boys.'

'The lot you deal with, or another lot?'

'I don't give a shit who they were. They were wearing balaclavas and they want it stopped. That's persuasion enough for me. And they're onto you. They said I was to give you a message, and you'd know what I was talking about. What are you going to do?'

'Wait. I'm thinking.'

Andy was silent for some time. Rory had been connected with the boys on two levels. The first was through Foley himself and the little cocaine business they had running; the second was through the funding of the shopping centre in Carrigraine. And, although the boys weren't normally shy about publicising their criminal activities, they would be reluctant to allow either of those projects to come to light. They liked to be seen as men of violence, men of action, responsible for acts that were heroic in their eyes. They wouldn't want it to be know that they had pettier interests than the liberation of the six counties, that on street level they were no more glorious than the average mugger or crooked alderman. For years now they had been controlling all the powder (the bikers controlled the resin), but they had been careful to make it seem that they were against drugs, going as far as executing anyone who tried to deal in Belfast itself. For them, stopping the investigation was a matter of saving face. And perhaps Fieselbaum had been right. Perhaps, after all, it was the boys who had sent Rory over the Black Rock. If that was the case, they had good reasons not to want an investigation. And McGrath had an even better reason. If the boys lost face he would be first in line for any reprisals.

He said, 'It'll be stopped. I don't know what the price will be, but it'll be stopped.'

The Characters Gather in the Drawing Room

The sun had gone to the other side of the Barrow and the heat of the day began to ebb. Patches of ragwort caught the light sideways on, losing their intensity as the blues and the whites came up and began to glow. Somewhere out at the back of the house Brendan was lost in contemplation of a teasel. He had forgotten about teasels, and had to think hard for the name of the plant when he saw this one. There was a fly drowning in one of the persistent wells of water at the leaf axils. The plant was not yet in flower, but he had a dim memory of diverging bands of mauve. From time to time he drew his finger along the line of prickles at the back of a leaf rib. There was a time when he would have drawn metaphors from the plant and bored everyone senseless with analogy, but now there wasn't the energy for new theories. Too often he had heard himself propound the old ideas again and again. They were beginning to sound implausible even to himself. It was a bit late now for self-doubt.

He became aware that two people were walking towards him. They came from the direction of the gate. He must have been spotted as they turned the first corner in the avenue. They consisted of a stout woman and a girl in pigtails. The woman walked slightly ahead, in a determined way, as if she had some important news for him. The girl moved in a more reluctant manner, as if she had walked a long way and was tired, and as if she were ashamed of something. As they drew near, the woman began to beam a great smile at him. She carried a leather satchel and wore incongruous training shoes. Both of them kept their hair in place with ordinary rubber bands. Having passed hailing distance, the woman said, 'Isn't it a lovely afternoon?'

Brendan wondered if they were from the press. Reporters had been coming and going all day. The guards had offered to put a man at the gate to keep them away, but Helen had refused, saying that she had nothing to hide from the press, and that she would prefer that her side of the story was printed along with everyone else's. This one certainly behaved like a reporter, with her smile fixed to her face as if she expected to be rebuffed at any second. And the girl was already looking back the way they had come with a certain longing, as if she would like to retreat before the rebuttal came.

He said, 'I suppose you want to ask questions.'

'Just a few,' she said, still beaming. 'You don't mind, do you?'

'Not at all,' he said. 'I'm used to it. Fire away.'

She took a clipboard out of her satchel, and a pen. 'Would you say,' she said, 'that you were a happy person?'

'Well,' he said, 'strictly within the context of your question, happiness is a term of such subjectivity that any direct answer would be as misleading as the question itself. On one hand, if we are to take a realistic view of a happiness as a temporary but recurring state of which a well-balanced individual is capable, the proper answer would be no, since if I were happy all the time I would be clinically insane. On the other hand, if I read the rather naive subtext of your question correctly, which has more to do with a general sense of contentment with the normal course of one's life, the answer, despite my present circumstances, is probably yes. Aren't you going to write any of this down? I wouldn't like to be misquoted. Would you like me to repeat it more slowly?'

The woman still smiled, but her eyes looked at him with blank incomprehension. Meanwhile, he was peering at the list of questions on her clipboard, his head pushed backwards in the attitude of the long-sighted, like a horse who has come above the bit. 'Oh, I see,' he said. 'I'm sorry. I thought you were a reporter. Which religion exactly are you from? Mormon? Jehovah's Witness?'

'Jehovah's Witness,' she said reluctantly, knowing from experience that to be unmasked so early in her sales pitch might well indicate that it was time to move on to the next household. The girl in pigtails, presumably her daughter, had winced at the admission and then seemed slightly relieved, as if the worst were over. She was standing to one side, her face reddening whenever Brendan looked in her direction.

'Ah yes,' he said enthusiastically, his face coming to life at the prospect of some meaty theological argument. 'I am, to some degree, in the same line of business myself.'

'You are a Witness?' the woman asked, with cautious incredulity. Her daughter seemed crestfallen.

'No, no,' he said, laughing. 'Far from it. I am the head of a movement which disseminates the doctrine of carnivorous atheism. But I am sure we have a lot to talk about. Do come up to the house. I'd like you to meet my wife.'

The woman had put away her clipboard and taken out her bible, every page of which was covered with underlinings and exclamation marks and annotations and day-glo highlightings. Her training had not equipped her to deal with this strange old man and she didn't know where to begin. She was hoping that the bible would fall open at the right page and supply her with an appropriate quotation, as it invariably did. It was difficult, however, to interrupt Brendan, who had begun a discourse on the psychology of proselytism. She allowed him to guide her towards the house, her daughter kicking at stones in their wake. He stopped by the medlar tree and pointed to an oak near the river.

'That is where we have just buried my son. I should have protested, of course. The whole thing runs against all my teachings. Flesh should be consumed. The Parsees have the right idea, although for completely the wrong reasons. You are familiar, of course, with Zoroastrianism? At the ashram, we leave the bodies of our dead brethren out in the jungle for the tigers to deal with. That, really, is a half-measure. If the doctrine were strictly adhered to, one should be consumed while still living. There you have my greatest dilemma. I should be the first to show an example, but who will carry on with the teaching once I am devoured? And now that I'm getting on a bit, there is the worry that I might die by natural causes. I'd be interested to hear what you think. The problem is academic while I am in this country, where there are no proper wild animals left to kill me. I suppose I could try one of the zoos. Tell me, do you think that the Christian habit of eating the flesh of Christ is a sublimation of our deeper carnivorous, not to say cannibalistic, desires? That reminds me of the Holy Grail for some reason. Did you know that it contained, not the blood of Christ, but his foreskin? It was the only part of him left on earth after the ascension, you see.'

The woman interrupted him with desperation in her voice. 'We should be going,' she said. 'It's getting late.'

'I wouldn't dream of letting you go,' he said. 'Come in for a cup of tea, at least.'

'We aren't allowed to drink tea.' It was the girl who spoke, but it wasn't clear whether the resentment in her voice was caused by his suggestion or if she would have liked to taste a cup of tea for once in her life. Either way, she was compelled to enter the house. Brendan, brooking no refusal, had led her mother by the arm through the back door and down the passage to the kitchen.

In other rooms within the house others came and went, seeming more focused on the issue of the day. Men with tweezers still ploughed the bathroom where Corinna had died, and in the small sitting room another man was cataloguing everything that had been found in the course of the day. In Rory's workroom Helen was having a difficult interview with Kieran Dunne, her solicitor. She had only required his presence so that he could advise her on how to handle the detectives' questions. Now he was telling her that she was poor, and probably homeless.

And she said, 'That's it, is it? I see. I might as well let them pin a few murders on me. At least if I go to prison I'll have a roof over my head. Perhaps I should just go straight out to them and confess everything. Is that what you want me to do?'

'Helen, look. I'm only telling you what I have to. It looks bad at the moment, but it isn't beyond hope. You have to talk to Dan and work something out. If we can get the banks to hold off for a while, who knows?'

'You had to tell me? Today? My entire family has been wiped out and today was the day for this? Who said you had to? Dan? So what's going on? Did the two of you work this out together so he could buy me out of the practice cheap?'

'Helen, for God's sake.'

'Don't for God's sake me. I know how these things work. Paint it as black as you can to begin with and then afterwards she'll be happy with enough money for a semi in Stillorgan, or some other suburban hellhole.'

'Helen, I'm trying to help. I know this isn't the best of times, but I should have told you all this last week, only Andy McGrath said you were too upset then.'

'Oh, McGrath's in on it too? I might have guessed.'

'For God's sake, no one is in on anything. Look. You are free to talk to the bank yourself, and see any accounts that you want to. But I have to say that if you are this unhappy about the way I am dealing with it you had better get another solicitor. I'd just like to say that I came here out of friendship, because the way Rory's estate looks at the moment I doubt if there's going to be a fee in it at the finish.'

'Well, if your fee is all you're worried about.'

He was about to protest when Brendan put his head round the door, saying, 'Has anyone seen Sheila? I can't find her anywhere. I have some friends who've just arrived. I was going to give them tea in the drawing room, if that's all right with you, Helen. They can't drink tea, of course, so they'll be having fruit juice, but there's tea for everyone else if you'd like to join us. I'm sure your young friend here would love to meet them, Helen. Bring him along if you like.'

When he had finished speaking he stared at them intensely for four seconds. It was a trick of his which had a profound effect on his disciples, but seemed to Kieran Dunne more like senile eccentricity. Then he passed his left hand through his bush of hair and quitted the room abruptly. It was difficult to think of anything to say in the vacuum left by him.

Eventually Kieran said, 'I think we've covered everything for the moment. You'll let me know whatever you decide. I'm sorry I'm not more help. I know these aren't the best of times for you.'

Helen had one forefinger between her lips and one forearm clutched across her chest, as if some uncomfortable realisation had come to her. Perhaps it was the spectacle of Brendan uttering his string of mad non sequiturs that had brought her to her senses.

'No,' she said. 'Stay. You might as well have a drink at least. You came so far. I shouldn't have spoken to you like that.'

'I don't mind. It can't be easy.'

'I don't know who to rely on,' she said. 'I never trusted anyone. Rory did it for me, and I never even trusted him. And I was right. He was not to be trusted. And I was wrong. I could have survived more easily by trusting him. And now I need to trust someone, badly. And I won't be able to. That isn't in me. Can you go on acting for me on the condition that I won't trust you?'

'I've done worse,' he said kindly.

'Well, then. We might as well go and see what Brendan has dragged into the drawing room.'

Sheila and Jody had already been in the drawing room for half an hour, playing detectives. They thought they had the whole thing worked out between them, and were debating whether they should bother to inform the real detectives of their theory. They agreed that if, as Sheila suspected, it was Andy McGrath who had killed Corinna, there was little chance of him ever being convicted of it. Sheila had seen Foley take the watch from the handbasin, had noticed McGrath's bare wrist, but there was nothing she could prove. And if Foley was covering for him there was no reason to suppose that the whole Department of Justice wasn't working to cover his tracks.

'But what was his motive?' Jody said. The game they were playing was unreal enough for him to suspend his emotional involvement. This was more like television than life.

'He didn't need a motive. He did it because he thought he could get away with it.' Sheila spoke as though she knew the man well, though she had only talked with him for a few minutes the day before.

'Everyone needs a motive.'

'Do they? Why? I very rarely see people do things for a motive. They invent motives afterwards. More often they do things because of who they are. Andy McGrath is a disgusting little man, so he will do disgusting things.'

'Perhaps it was him who made the first cut? Perhaps Corinna knew that?'

Sheila shook her head. 'Cutting the brake cable was an act of stupidity. McGrath might be a lot of things, but not stupid. Whether it was done as a warning or whether it was intended to kill, there was an equal chance that it would have backfired. Whoever cut the cable was dim and desperate.'

'That would sum up most of us.'

It was at that point that Brendan came in carrying a vast wooden tray, followed by his Jehovah's Witnesses.

'You're already here,' he said. 'Good. I was looking for you.' He set the tray down on the stainless steel coffee table that was suspended by wires from the ceiling. 'I'd like you to meet Patsy and Rebecca. This is my wife, Sheila, and her friend. Sorry, I don't know your name.'

'Jody,' Jody said.

'Patsy and I were just talking about transubstantiation. The juice is for them. Unless, Jody, you don't drink tea either?'

'No, tea is fine.'

Brendan seemed a little disappointed by Jody's manifestation of normality, but not disappointed enough to cease telling Sheila what Patsy thought of transubstantiation. Patsy and Rebecca sat primly on the same armchair, Patsy in the seat and Rebecca on the arm, Patsy trying to smile at everyone at once and Rebecca counting the stitches in the weave of her skirt. They were joined by Kieran Dunne and Helen, who said, 'Good God, I may be a pauper, but there's still gin in the house. Jody, what are you doing here?'

'I thought it was time I came,' he said. At the sight of Helen he was in danger of coming down again, after the euphoria of the afternoon. He wanted Rory to be there, and he wanted to cry.

'Pauper?' Sheila said.

Helen turned to Kieran and said, 'You tell her. You might as well tell everyone. Poverty and riches can never be hid, as Rory used to say. Not that he made a bad job of it himself.'

'I think,' Kieran said, 'that maybe this isn't the moment. Perhaps I could have a word with you later, Mrs Dixon, about your son's estate.'

The sofa which Sheila and Jody sat on had a high back and faced away from the door, so that when Kay came into the room, after the drinks had been poured, she did not notice her husband at first.

'What's going on?' she said, seeing so many people there. 'I didn't mean to come, but I found David Kennedy walking the road out from Gavinston. He said he was coming here, so I gave him a lift. He said something about the trees in the avenue. He's out there now. I didn't know if you'd want him there, so I thought I should tell you.' She said all this in an apologetic flood, and then she said, 'Oh Jesus,' and began to sob. Kieran put his arm around her, and Jody watched his wife over the top of the sofa, like a hidden child who doesn't want to be found and taken home.

Brendan was looking from Helen to Kay and back again, and said in an excitable way, 'Has anyone noticed how alike those two women are? Practically twins.'

No one seemed to take any notice of him except Jody, who realised that there was some truth in it. It was only knowing them both so well which had pre-

vented him from seeing the similarities before. And
that his wife was as sane as Helen was mad. That was
it. It must be Kay's anguished face which made her
look even more like Helen. Perhaps, he thought, that
was why Rory used to sleep with Kay, because she was
a sane version of the woman he loved.

'Jody's gone,' Kay was saying. 'The priest said he
rowed off in the boat. I've been driving up and down
the roads to see if he was still out on the water. Oh,
Jesus help me if he's drowned.'

'I'm not,' Jody said resentfully, and braced himself
as she flew at him with as much force as affection
can fuel.

'Where is David Kennedy now?' Sheila asked, rising
to be out of the way of the O'Driscolls' impact.

Helen said, 'The little snot is probably hanging himself. He would do it here, just to annoy us.'

Anyone else would have thrown her a sharp look,
but Sheila only laid her hand on the woman's bony
braceleted arm, on her way to the door.

'I'll go to him,' she said.

In the doorway she passed the two detectives on
their way in. They were a little taken aback by the
number of people in the room, but the first one recovered himself to say, 'It's just as well you're all here.
There's a few things we'd like to clear up.'

Helen stood closer to Kieran. 'This is my solicitor,'
she said, with something like defiance.

'It's yourself,' the first detective said. 'Howiyah,
Kieran.'

'Howiyah, Jim,' Kieran said, with what Helen considered to be unwarranted friendliness.

She recoiled from him. 'I don't fucking believe it,'
she said. 'Are there any two people who don't know
each other in this arsehole of a country?'

Patsy, being a Witness, stood up. She didn't see that
there was any call for that sort of language. As far as

204

she was concerned the only reason the bible didn't specifically forbid anyone to say 'Fuck' was that the word was too profane to be included in the book. There was no mention, as far as she could remember, of arseholes either. She held her bible out in front of her and shouted, 'The wages of sins is damnation. We should all pray for forgiveness.'

Her daughter was edging towards the door, with a face the colour of blood.

'Sin, surely,' Helen said.

'Can we be sure?' Brendan said. 'It may well be the other way round, with those who have learned to have a good time on earth being rewarded with an even better time in heaven. Not, of course, that I believe in heaven.'

'I do,' Jody said.

And then a telephone rang somewhere in the house, and a uniformed garda came in and whispered in the ear of the first detective, and the first detective left the room with a concerned look on his face.

Sheila returned with David. He had a frightened look to him, too confused to have disobeyed Sheila by not coming in with her.

'Have we had the denouncement yet?' Sheila said. 'I haven't had excitement like this for years. Has anyone got a joint on them?'

Patsy crossed herself, in her horror forgetting for a moment that she was now a Witness, and reverting to her original Catholicism. She realised that she had to get Rebecca out of this den of sinners quickly before they became tainted, but when she looked about her Rebecca was already gone.

The detective returned.

'Well,' he said, 'we'll be saying goodnight to you.'

'I thought you had questions to ask,' Jody said.

'No. You're all right there. There'll be no more of that for the moment.'

'But,' Sheila said. 'We can tell you who did it. Jody and I worked the whole thing out.'

'Not now,' the detective said. 'We've been recalled, in the interests of national security.'

Dixie Chicken

Since there is no hell, the devil has to walk on earth, but the less said about him the better. In some ways I am not as well qualified as some of his other apologists – as Milton or the Rolling Stones – to discuss him. I look for his work, but from this distance it is hard to distinguish his work from yours or mine. If we who are trying to do good have such mixed results and create so much evil, then cannot he be a creator of much that is good, despite himself?

After the farce in the drawing room, after the guards and detectives had vanished in dark blue cars, after the Jehovah's Witnesses had disappeared down the drive – mother scampering on the trail of her daughter – after David Kennedy had gone God-knew-where (to stand beneath the darkening chestnut trees and think lovingly about hanging himself from the branches beneath which he had first seen Corinna, before walking back to Gavinston in his impotence), after Kieran Dunne had gone to his cottage in Fethard rather than spend an evening being grilled about a complicated legal situation on which most of his advice would only be conjecture, after Kay had gone back to the Commodore Hotel alone, having elicited promises from Jody that he would follow her later (promises she knew he wouldn't keep – something was destroyed between them, and it would take more than kind behaviour and good intentions to restore it), after the light had turned to indigo in the dusk, the four who remained sat in silence and lamplight.

The silence, at first, was a companionable relief from the earlier discord, but silence between four people is soon burdensome so Sheila said, 'I don't know about anyone else, but I'm starving.'

Her voice broke over them, sounding unnaturally loud, and they looked at her slyly as if her suggestion of food had contained an element of obscenity, and just as the silence had closed on them again Brendan said quietly, 'What's the point?'

'Why? Aren't you hungry?'

'Yes. But I don't see the point of eating. I have been eating for seventy-eight years. Imagine how much food that is. Rooms and rooms full.' He did some calculations in his head. 'A horse pond full of excrement. What's the point?'

'Oh, for God's sake,' Helen said. 'You don't make yourself sound less banal by being vulgar. Grow up.'

Again, anyone else would have leapt to her husband's defence on hearing him being spoken to like a child, anyone else would have at least thrown Helen a look of reproof, but Sheila only laid her hand on the woman's arm and said nothing. And Brendan was smiling at them, and said, 'You're right, you know. We might as well eat. I'll give you a hand.'

Brendan and Sheila went to the kitchen where they carved cold ham left from the funeral, and sliced potatoes and grated cheese to make a dauphinoise. As Sheila chopped the garlic she said, 'I want to stay here. I won't be going back.'

'I know,' he said.

'I talked to that solicitor just before he left. Helen hasn't a bean. The houses will have to be sold.'

'Is that enough meat?' he said.

'I suppose we could buy this house. She won't be

easy to live with, but she can't be worse than some of the disciples.'

'I like her,' he said.

'Do you? So do I. There aren't many of us. When I first saw her I couldn't understand how Rory put up with her, but I can see now that no one else would have put up with him. They would in theory, but she was the only one who was capable of it in practice. She's very strong. A bit battered maybe, but he never broke her. I think he knew what he was doing.'

'Will I put it on four plates or on one big plate?' he said.

'I used to hear other people worrying about their children, but I never worried about him. Did you?'

'Maybe one big plate is better,' he said.

'You don't mind? Not going back.'

'I mind,' he said. 'I never wanted to come, but I knew from the start we would never go back. I mind a lot, but it's over now. I know you're right. I'm not stupid.'

'I know,' she said. 'Brendan?' she said. 'While we're waiting for the potatoes to cook, we could do it.'

'Here?' he said.

'Here,' she said. 'They won't be interrupting us.'

She put her garlic-impregnated fingers to his face and pushed the folds until his eyes were shut, and kissed him on the mouth.

'Can you tell me something?' she said. 'I don't smell old, do I?'

'I wouldn't know,' he said. 'If you do, I do, and I wouldn't notice.'

He put his nose to her neck and inhaled, and she let her chin rest on top of his head. 'I think,' he said, 'you still smell of yourself.'

The feeling between Helen and Jody, after they had been left alone, was almost one of embarrassment, of something like nakedness. They both knew what was going to happen, and they were both thinking of reasons to prevent it happening, and at the same time looking for ways to make it happen more naturally, manoeuvres or words that would make it seem accidental. It was he who put his arms around her, because she seemed so brittle that he thought she was going to cry. It was she who put her mouth to his, because she could feel his legs shaking against her own. They were a long time kissing and their kissing was hungry, and when they had been dulled by the kissing to everything save for the need in each for the skin of the other, they went upstairs in unspoken agreement. She wouldn't have known which room to take him to, but he opened the door of the spare room where he had been most often with Rory, and that was where they undressed, each watching the skin of the other as it was unclothed, and then they kissed again for a long time until they were too weak from kissing not to fuck.

There was no art or artifice or technique or skilled gymnastics. It was that act of mutual desperation which can never be simulated, the forces in which are too great for it to be called a pleasure, the climax of which is a weeping dissolution rather than a coloured thrill, the aftermath of which is the relief of having survived it rather than smug well-being. It was a long time of clinging before a word could be spoken that would not be awkward or trite or hang in the air until it crumbled for want of meaning.

She looked into both his eyes and said, 'Why?'

He said, 'Why anything? I can only answer half of it and guess your half. I don't like things unfinished and this is the finish of something.'

'And my half?'

'For things you don't know. You'll never be yourself until you know the parts of him he hid from you. Because you loved Rory.'

'You're wrong,' she said. 'You guessed wrong. Rory

wasn't the man I loved. I think now he was, after all, the man I feared he was. If I gave him a bad time it was because I didn't want to believe what I should have known: that my instinct was right. If I had known for sure I would have left him long ago.'

'Wasn't it your instincts made you stay with him?'

'I don't know,' she said. 'All I know is that I lost myself somewhere while I was trying to fathom him, and I should have known that his love was all pretence.'

'You're wrong,' he said. He screwed his eyes as if it hurt him to talk. 'You're wrong. You're wrong. He could never pretend anything. He was as honest in his infidelity as he was honest in his love for you. He wasn't good and he wasn't bad. He was like a conduit, and good and bad could flow through him. If it seemed that evil was flowing through him it was only that there was so much evil around him. People know nothing.'

She looked at Jody sharply across the pillow. 'That was his expression,' she said.

'I know,' he said. 'He said it to me the day he died.'

'What?'

'And you were wrong about something else. Rory could not have been murdered. There is no power on this earth that could have put an end to his life. There were people who wanted him dead, but none who could have brought it about.'

'When did you see him?' she said. 'You never told anyone.'

'Told anyone what? That I was in bed with him an hour before he died? If they had wanted to know they could have found out anyway. He died with my fluid still inside him.'

'Oh, Jesus, no,' she said. She didn't know whether to cling to him for comfort or push him away in disgust. 'Why?'

'Why go to bed with anyone? You have to take love where you can get it. What do you think we were doing

211

just now? Is sleeping with you morally superior to sleeping with your husband?'

'Jesus Christ,' she said.

'These days,' he said, 'safe sex is sex with the people you know.'

At the sound of a sob breaking from her he said, 'I'm sorry. That was unkind. That was unnecessary. That was untrue.'

At the same moment, something broke out of the two of them that could have been a sob, but it wasn't. It was the beginnings of an inexplicable laughter. It was a mixture of hysteria and desperation and amusement. As it subsided he said, 'That must be why death isn't so terrible. If you found yourself in heaven you'd be fine, and if you found yourself in hell you'd break your arse laughing.'

She was still pulsing against him with the wake of the laughter, waking a desire in him to fuck again, but this time there was no desperation or urgency. He held his erection close to her while they spoke.

'Did you love him?' she said.

'Yes.'

'And Rory?'

'He made me think there was love in it. It isn't for me to say. We enjoyed ourselves, and I always left it at that. Oddly enough, it was always me that did it to him. You'd think, wouldn't you, knowing Rory, him being such a man and all, that it would have been the other way around. He said it was like dying. He said that when I was inside of him he thought he was going to die, like his body was being rent apart. I think he liked the idea of dying now and again. I think that was where the pleasure was.'

They were both talking in calm voices now, as if they were discussing something ordinary, she stroking him with the affection of long-time lovers, the curiosity in her questions no more than the curiosity of normal conversation.

212

'Do you know how he died?' she said.

'Yes.'

'How?'

'I saw it. I was standing on the headland and I saw it. When he came to me that day his brakes had already been cut. I don't know who did that, but he got them mended at the garage in Knockjames. He seemed very calm about it, as if it was a joke. We were in Dermot Little's cottage. Dermot gave me the key so I could water his plants.

'I think that Rory always had some kind of death wish. All that bravery wasn't courage, it was curiosity. That day, he said that maybe he had outlived his time; he said that maybe he had done everything that was possible, and it wouldn't be a bad thing to die before he went into decline. At any other time I would have thought he was joking. Another time I would have thought that it was the coke talking.

'We were talking about love.'

Jody's voice faded at the end of the sentence. She could hear that his breathing was sharper when he inhaled, as though he was making some kind of effort to keep control of himself until he had finished what he had to say.

He said, 'I should have known, but I don't know if I could have stopped it. I pushed him hard. I don't know that I had ever seen him in that state before. I don't think he had ever been in that state before. It didn't seem possible that there should be despair on that face, and when I saw it I pushed harder still, trying to break him. And then he was angry. Angry for the first time because he had seen fear for the first time.

'When everything seemed normal again we left the house together. He opened the bonnet of the Spider to show me the cut in the brakes. It was all jokes again by this stage, but I saw that something was changed in him. He did the second cut himself, making it seem no more than an act of bravado. I thought he was just trying to prove that he wasn't afraid after all.

'It was when he drove away, and turned left up the headland instead of right for Innish, that I knew what was going to happen. I started running across the fields. I don't know what I thought I could do to stop it. I got to the place above the Black Rock just as the Spider was coming down the hill towards it. He must have been accelerating. He needn't have bothered to cut the brakes at all. That was just for my benefit.

'Do you remember? I don't know if he ever told you, but he said it to me often. He always said that he wanted to die while listening to that Little Feat song. I swear I could hear that song on the wind as the car went over the cliff.'

' "Dixie Chicken",' she said.

She separated herself from him and got out of bed, reaching for her clothes and drawing them on with an awkward modesty, as if the intimacy between them had long been broken. 'They'll be wondering where we got to,' she said. 'We should eat.' She was speaking in a voice which he had never heard before, sounding for the first time as if she wasn't under attack. He wondered if an exorcism was that simple, if he wasn't only imagining a change in her as a reflection of the change in himself.

Since there is no nell, the devil has to walk on earth, but he is old now and living on handouts. He may stand at the foot of your bed, and he may frighten you, but he is no longer in a position to bargain for your soul. He has nothing to offer you which you cannot take with your own two hands. There is worse to be feared than the devil, who after all is no worse than I made him.

A Hero's Death

Under the circumstances there was nothing I could do, and there is nothing I can do now. You who have sex and alcohol and conversation to staunch your wounds are relatively lucky. In bereavement you can always hope to meet the dead in the next world. I, inhabiting the next world, know already who has come here and who has been denied entrance. Too often it is those whose company I want the most who are excluded. Socrates is not here, nor is Van Gogh, nor Ian Curtis, nor Primo Levi, nor Rory Dixon.

I feel old now, and I am old. It may pass. I have felt old at other times and got over it, but these sensations of ageing are cumulative, and there must come a time when there will be no remission. The telling of this story has made things seem a little better. Tomorrow there will be more birth, more chances for a reason to continue. But I don't know that I can bear to go through this again. The first time you fall in love you are miserable, because you feel you will never survive it. The second and maybe the third time you can be happy, because you know that love will not overcome you completely. There comes a point, however, when you don't have the energy or the spirit any more, when you don't believe any more that the love you feel will be genuine, because love depends on innocence and you are no longer innocent, and you know that

215

you will be loving only for the sake of addiction. I honestly believe at this moment that Rory Dixon was the last I could love.

Not that there aren't others crying out for it. There is Alan Kehoe in a workers' hostel in London, temporarily relieved by the taciturnity of the city. There is Jody O'Driscoll holding himself responsible for the death of his lover, being steadily hardened by his guilt. There is Helen who, as her terrors fall away, will find that nothing remains, and will have to seek new terrors, new love.

Who can say for certain why he did it? I know what he was thinking and I know the reasons he gave himself, but that thinking and those reasons were no more in substance than the abstract thoughts of suicide that anyone can have at any time, thoughts and reasons which in themselves bring relief and remove the necessity to commit the act.

Jody did not tell the whole truth, nor could he. He imagined, that morning when Rory arrived at Dermot Little's cottage, that his life was under control. He knew that he loved Rory, but he thought that he could contain that love, could resist spoiling the pleasure between them with his emotion. And then Rory joked about the cut in the brake cable. He began to speculate about who would like to see him dead.

Quietly Jody said, 'Anyone would.'

And Rory didn't know if he was being serious, although there had been a frightening calm and purpose in his voice, and Rory laughed just in case.

Jody said, 'I would. I would kill you now if I could.'

And Rory asked why.

'Because I can't see any other way of reaching you. When I am inside you, and you feel as though you are dying, that is the closest we get. Because you are afraid of nothing. Not even afraid of being unloved, and so you are easily loved, but loving you is a deep black hole with no sides and no end. Loving you is loving no one, and loving you will make no sense until you are dead.'

It was not so much the words but how they were spoken, and who had spoken them. Rory said, 'Snap out of it, for Christ's sake. This is the last thing I need. Have a toot.' He said those words, but his voice had a rare taint of uncertainty, and his face was changed.

Jody saw what was on his face, and pushed on; his quarry, if it existed, was somewhere in Rory's despair. He told him what it was like not to be Rory Dixon and to know Rory Dixon. There was little in what he said which had not been said by Helen before, as well as by others, but now it was being said with an unnerving calmness of voice and had the ring of truth to it. And it was reinforced by the cut cable in the Spider outside, and by being said by Jody, who was without malice or duplicity, and who could have no motive, only the expression of what could no longer be contained.

Rory Dixon felt a rage inside of him. He knew that he was the best that could be, and still his life was presented to him as a chasm of failure. He folded over on himself and rocked like a madman, as if he could burst the life out of himself with torsion, and still the quiet voice went on.

It ended in an embrace of course, and sex followed, naturally, but this time Rory wept in the cadence of penetration. He said to himself, in such a low voice that Jody misheard it, 'I'll leave it to God.'

How could he have called on me? He had never for a moment questioned his disbelief in my existence. Perhaps it was just an expression. Perhaps he meant that he would leave it to fate, but he used my name as others have at times when I could be of no help to them. My will is rarely done, and I don't have the power to take the cup away.

So he cut the brake himself, and so I lost him. I don't

217

know where the suicides go. I only know that they don't come here. If I had a mortal life myself, it is a thing I might do, just to find out. He put that song on the stereo – the one he had always said he would die to, the song about Dixie Chickens and Tennessee Lambs – and turned the volume up full, and the car sailed out over the cliff in an arc of music.

He is gone on me and I can't get him back. I am only God and I didn't make the rules.